GEPT 新制全民英檢
初級 閱讀實戰力 Level Up!

詳解本

Contents 目錄

Chapter 1 單篇閱讀 ▶ Part A 文章類

Chapter 1 單篇閱讀 ▶ Part B 生活類

全民英檢 初級 簡答表

U1

• 段落填空

1. C	2. D	3. B	4. A

• 閱讀理解

1. A	2. D	3. C

U2

• 段落填空

1. D	2. B	3. A	4. C

• 閱讀理解

1. A	2. D	3. A

U3

• 段落填空

1. A	2. B	3. D	4. C

• 閱讀理解

1. D	2. C	3. B

U4

• 段落填空

1. D	2. C	3. A	4. D

• 閱讀理解

1. A	2. D	3. A

U5

• 段落填空

1. B	2. C	3. D	4. A

• 閱讀理解

1. C	2. D	3. D

U6

• 段落填空

1. D	2. B	3. A	4. C

• 閱讀理解

1. C	2. A	3. A

U7

• 段落填空

1. B	2. D	3. C	4. A

• 閱讀理解

1. A	2. C	3. D

U8

• 段落填空

1. C	2. D	3. B	4. A

• 閱讀理解

1. A	2. C	3. B

U9

• 段落填空

1. C	2. A	3. D	4. B

• 閱讀理解

1. C	2. D	3. D

U10

• 段落填空

1. D	2. C	3. A	4. B

• 閱讀理解

1. A	2. B	3. C

U11

A

1. C	2. B	3. C

B

1. C	2. D	3. A

U12

A

1. D	2. A	3. B

B

1. C	2. A	3. B

U13

A

1. A	2. B	3. D

B

1. C	2. D	3. C

U14

A

1. C	2. B	3. C

B

1. C	2. A	3. C

U15

A

1. B	2. C	3. D

B

1. C	2. B	3. C

U16

A

1. D	2. B	3. C

B

1. A	2. C	3. C

U17

A

1. A	2. A	3. B

B

1. A	2. C	3. D

U18

A

1. D	2. B	3. A

B

1. A	2. B	3. A

U19

A

1. A	2. A	3. C

B

1. A	2. D	3. C

U20

A

1. B	2. D	3. C

B

1. B	2. A	3. C

U21		
1. C	2. D	3. D

U31		
1. C	2. A	3. B

U22		
1. C	2. A	3. C

U32		
1. C	2. D	3. D

U23		
1. B	2. C	3. B

U33		
1. C	2. B	3. C

U24		
1. A	2. D	3. D

U34		
1. D	2. C	3. C

U25		
1. C	2. B	3. C

U35		
1. B	2. A	3. C

U26		
1. B	2. D	3. A

U36		
1. D	2. C	3. C

U27		
1. D	2. B	3. B

U37		
1. B	2. C	3. C

U28		
1. A	2. A	3. D

U38		
1. D	2. A	3. C

U29		
1. D	2. C	3. B

U39		
1. A	2. D	3. C

U30		
1. B	2. D	3. B

U40		
1. B	2. D	3. A

Chapter 1 單篇閱讀 詳解

Part A 文章類

Diet & Health 飲食與健康

段落填空

Bananas are eaten all over the world because they are delicious, healthy, and convenient. Usually, people only eat the _(1)_ of a banana. They throw away the peel, which is the yellow or green skin on the outside of the banana. _(2)_ This is because it contains many things _(3)_ are good for our blood sugar and heart health. Eating the skin also _(4)_ less waste. Banana skins, though, may contain bad chemicals. This means they must be washed very carefully before they are eaten. Baking or boiling them is a good idea, too. Even after cooking the skins, they may still be hard and taste bitter.

全世界的人都吃香蕉，因為它好吃、有益健康而且簡便。一般人通常只吃香蕉的<u>內部</u>。大家會把外皮 —— 也就是黃色或綠色的香蕉外層 —— 丟棄。<u>然而有些人主張我們也該吃香蕉皮</u>。這是因為香蕉皮含有許多對血糖及心臟健康有益的物質。吃香蕉皮的話，<u>產生</u>的廢棄物也較少。不過香蕉皮可能含有不好的化學物質。這表示香蕉皮必須仔細清洗後才能吃下肚。把香蕉皮烘烤或用沸水煮也是個好主意。但即便經過烹煮，香蕉皮的口感可能還是偏硬且嚐起來帶苦味。

C **1.**

ⓐ A. **image** [ˈɪmɪdʒ] *n.* 形象；意象；影像，圖像

▶ The team is trying to improve the company's image.
這個團隊正在設法改善公司的形象。

B. **addition** [əˈdɪʃən] *n.* 添加；加法

▶ The addition of the spice to this dish makes it taste better.
在這道菜裡添加這種香料會讓它更美味。

C. **inside** [ˈɪnˈsaɪd] *n.* 內部

▶ We couldn't open the door because it was locked from the inside.
我們無法把門打開，因為門從裡面上鎖了。

D. **surface** [ˈsɝfɪs] *n.* 表面

▶ There are a lot of leaves floating on the surface of the lake.
湖面上漂浮著許多樹葉。

ⓑ 根據上述，C 項應為正選。

D **2.**

ⓐ A. Bananas are now in danger from illness.
香蕉現在因為某種疫病而面臨危機。

B. Banana skins, though, create a lot of trash.
但香蕉皮是大量的垃圾。

C. Yet, we should eat many different kinds of fruit.
不過我們應該吃多種不同的水果。

D. However, some people say that we should eat the skin, too.
然而有些人主張我們也該吃香蕉皮。

ⓑ 前句提及 "They throw away the peel..."（大家會把外皮……丟棄），而後句敘述 "This is because it contains many things that are good for our blood sugar and heart health."（這是因為香蕉皮含有許多對血糖以及心臟健康有益的物質。），D 項置入空格後符合前後文語意，故應為正選。

B 3.

ⓐ 空格前為完整句子 "it contains many things..."（香蕉皮含有許多……物質），空格後為 be 動詞 are 及形容詞 good，得知空格應置關係代名詞 which / that，引導形容詞子句修飾先行詞 many things。

ⓑ 根據上述，B 項應為正選。

A 4.

ⓐ A. **lead to...**　　導致……
= result in...
（lead 的動詞三態為：lead, led [lɛd], led）
▶ The typhoon led to a power failure throughout the city.
這場颱風導致全市停電。

B. **take away... / take... away**　　帶走……
（take 的動詞三態為：take, took [tʊk], taken [ˈtekən]）
▶ Mike was angry because Rita took his toys away without telling him.
麥克很生氣，因為麗塔沒跟他說就拿走他的玩具。

C. **make up...**　　組成……；編造（故事、藉口等）
（make 的動詞三態為：make, made [med], made）
▶ It takes nine people to make up a baseball team.
組成一支棒球隊需要九個人。

D. **deal with sb/sth**　　與某人打交道；處理某事
（deal 的動詞三態為：deal, dealt [dɛlt], dealt）
▶ Jodie can't come to the party because she has to deal with some personal matters.
裘蒂不能來參加派對，因為她得處理一些私人事務。

ⓑ 根據上述，A 項應為正選。

🏷 重要單字片語

1. **healthy** [ˈhɛlθɪ] *a.* 有益健康的；健康的
   health [hɛlθ] *n.* 健康
2. **peel** [pil] *n.* 水果皮
3. **contain** [kənˈten] *vt.* 包含；裝有
4. **blood sugar**　血糖
5. **waste** [west] *n.* 廢棄物（不可數）
6. **chemical** [ˈkɛmɪkḷ] *n.* 化學製品（可數）
7. **boil** [bɔɪl] *vt. & vi.*（使）沸騰
8. **bitter** [ˈbɪtɚ] *a.*（味道）苦的
9. **(be) in danger**　有危險

📖 閱讀理解

Eggs Benedict is a popular breakfast and brunch food. It is made with a round, flat bread called an English muffin, which is cut in half. Eggs and Canadian bacon are two other main elements. Finally, it is topped with hollandaise, which is a mix of eggs, butter, and lemon juice. The history of eggs Benedict can be traced back to the US in the 19th century. However, there are different opinions as to who invented the dish. Some say that a woman named Mrs. Benedict asked the cook at a New York restaurant to create something new for her in the 1860s. Others say that a man named Lemuel Benedict first ordered all the elements for eggs Benedict in a New York hotel in 1894. Whatever the truth of the matter is, eggs Benedict is enjoyed in lots of countries today. You can now also order many special types, which include everything from tomatoes and potatoes to fish.

火腿蛋鬆餅（班尼迪克蛋）是一種受歡迎的早餐及早午餐。製作時要用到名為英式鬆餅的扁圓形麵包，將其對半橫切。另外兩種主要食材是蛋和加拿大培根。最後在上方淋上荷蘭醬，是混合了蛋、奶油和檸檬汁的一種醬汁。火腿蛋鬆餅的歷史可以追溯至十九世紀的美國。不過關於這道料理的發明者是誰，有多種不同說法。有人說在 1860 年代，有一位班尼迪克太太請紐約某間餐廳的廚師為她做一道新的料理。另有人說在 1894 年，一位名叫萊謬爾・班尼迪克的男子在紐約一間飯店首次點了包含火腿蛋鬆餅所有食材的餐點。不論真相是什麼，現在火腿蛋鬆餅在許多國家都很受歡迎。你現在也可以點選許多特製的種類，包括番茄、洋芋乃至於魚肉應有盡有。

A **1.** Which of the following would be the best title for the article?
   A. *The Story of a Popular Dish*
   B. *The Best Ways to Cook Eggs*
   C. *The Finest Brunches in the US*
   D. *The Favorite Foods of Mr. Benedict*

下列哪一項最適合做為本文的標題？
A. 一道熱門料理的故事
B. 料理蛋類的最佳方法
C. 美國的最佳早午餐點
D. 班尼迪克先生最喜愛的食物

理由

問題類型：　主旨題

本文第一至四句介紹火腿蛋鬆餅（班尼迪克蛋）包含的材料，第五至八句敘述其起源的不同說法，最後兩句說明此料理的現況，得知 A 項應為正選。

D **2.** When was eggs Benedict first created?
- A. In a hotel in 1860
- B. In a restaurant in 1894
- C. In Canada in the 1900s
- D. We don't know for sure.

火腿蛋鬆餅最早是在什麼時候發明的？
- A. 1860 年在一間飯店中
- B. 1894 年在一間餐廳裡
- C. 1900 年代間在加拿大
- D. 無法確知。

理由

問題類型：　推論題

本文第五至八句敘述火腿蛋鬆餅的起源眾說紛紜，並列舉其中兩個說法，可知真正的起源無人知曉，故 D 項應為正選。

C **3.** What is true of eggs Benedict?
- A. It is only made with bacon and eggs.
- B. It is only eaten in the United States.
- C. It is now available in different types.
- D. It is no longer as popular as it once was.

哪一項關於火腿蛋鬆餅的敘述是正確的？
- A. 只用培根和蛋做成。
- B. 只有在美國有人吃。
- C. 現在有各種不同的種類。
- D. 現在不像以前那樣受歡迎。

理由

問題類型：　細節題

根據本文最後一句 "You can now also order many special types, which include everything from tomatoes and potatoes to fish."（你現在也可以點選許多特製的種類，包括番茄、洋芋乃至於魚肉應有盡有。），得知 C 項應為正選。

🏷 **重要單字片語**

1. **brunch** [brʌntʃ] *n.* 早午餐（由 breakfast 與 lunch 兩字結合而成）

2. **muffin** [ˋmʌfɪn] *n.* 鬆餅
   an English muffin　英式鬆餅

3. **in half**　一分為二

4. **element** [ˋɛləmənt] *n.* 組成部分；要素

5. **be topped with...**　在朝上的表面放上……

6. **hollandaise** [ˏhɑlənˋdez] / [ˋhɑlənˏdez] *n.* 荷蘭醬

7. **be traced back to...**　追溯至……

8 **as to...**　關於……

9. **invent** [ɪnˋvɛnt] *vt.* 發明

10. **available** [əˋveləbl̩] *a.* 可得到的；可利用的；有空的

Unit 2

Sports & Fitness 運動與健身

段落填空

Not everyone likes to take part in organized team sports. Some people (1) to build exercise into their daily lives. One way to do this in Taipei, and other big cities in Taiwan, is to use a YouBike. This bicycle sharing service started in 2009. It allows people (2) a bicycle from one station and return it to any other station. This means it is very convenient. It is also very cheap and easy to use. (3) , too, as they are made by the respected Taiwanese company Giant. The YouBike system helps people to fit exercise into their day. (4) , they can ride a bicycle to or from school or work.

不是每個人都喜歡參與有組織的團體運動。有些人比較喜歡把運動當成日常生活的一部分。在臺北和臺灣其他大城市要做到這一點，其中一種方式就是使用 YouBike（微笑單車）。這項自行車共享服務始於 2009 年。它讓人們能在某個車站租一臺自行車，然後在任何其他車站歸還。這意味它是個很便利的服務。它也非常便宜且使用簡單。這些自行車的品質也很好，因為它們是由極具聲望的臺灣公司捷安特所製造。YouBike 系統有助於人們將運動融入日常生活。例如他們可以騎單車上下學或上下班。

D **1.**

ⓐ A. **pause** [pɔz] *vi.* 停頓，暫停

　　pause to V　　停頓片刻來做……

▶ Howard paused to think about his answer.
　 霍華德停頓了一下，思考他的答案。

B. **promise** [ˋprɑmɪs] *vi.* 答應，承諾

　　promise to V　　答應／允諾做……

▶ Stacy promised to take care of our children for us while we were away.
　 我們不在時，史黛西答應為我們照顧孩子。

C. **progress** [prəˋgrɛs] *vi.* 進行，進展

　　progress to + N/V-ing　　逐步發展到……

▶ Joan started jogging in the park and progressed to running long-distance races.
　 瓊安一開始在公園裡慢跑，然後逐漸進步到參加長途賽跑。

D. **prefer** [prɪˋfɝ] *vt.* 比較喜歡，偏好

　　prefer to V　　較喜歡／偏好做……

▶ Comedies aren't my cup of tea. I prefer to watch action films.
　 喜劇片不是我的菜。我比較喜歡看動作片。

ⓑ 根據語意及用法，得知 D 項應為正選。

<u>B</u> **2.**

ⓐ 空格前有及物動詞 allow（允許），得知本空格測試下列固定用法：

allow sb to V 允許某人做……

▸ Beth's mother doesn't allow her to eat snacks between meals.
貝絲的媽媽不准她在兩餐之間吃零食。

ⓑ 根據上述，B 項應為正選。

<u>A</u> **3.**

ⓐ A. The bicycles are of good quality
這些自行車的品質很好

B. Running is an easy decision
跑步是個簡單的決定

C The service stops on weekends
這項服務每逢週末暫停

D. You should maintain your health
你應該保持健康

ⓑ 根據本文第四句 "This bicycle sharing service started in 2009."（這項自行車共享服務始於 2009 年。）及本句後半句 "as they are made by the respected Taiwanese company Giant"（因為它們是由極具聲望的臺灣公司捷安特所製造），可推知空格應與自行車有關，A 項置入空格後符合上下文語意，故應為正選。

<u>C</u> **4.**

ⓐ A. **at last** 終於，最後

▸ At last, the movie star has arrived at the award ceremony.
那位電影明星終於到達了頒獎典禮現場。

B. **until now** 直到現在（與表否定意味的現在完成式或現在完成進行式並用）

▸ Jason has not been able to contact his father until now.
傑森直到現在才聯絡上他父親。

C. **for example** 例如，舉例來說

= for instance

▸ John loves outdoor activities. For example, he enjoys hiking and fishing.
約翰喜歡戶外活動。例如，他喜歡健行及釣魚。

D. **on the contrary** 相反地

▸ Everyone thinks Terry is lazy, but on the contrary, he is a hard worker.
所有人都認為泰瑞很懶惰，但相反地，他其實很努力工作。

ⓑ 根據空格前一句 "The YouBike system helps people to fit exercise into their day."（YouBike 系統有助於人們將運動融入日常生活。）及空格後的句子 "they can ride a bicycle to or from school or work"（他們可以騎單車上下學或上下班），可推知空格後的句子應是在為空格前一句舉例說明，C 項置入空格符合上下文語意，故應為正選。

📑 重要單字片語

1. **take part in...**　　參與……
= participate in...
2. **organized** [ˈɔrgəˌnaɪzd] *a.* 有組織的
3. **build A into B**　　使 A 成為 B 的一部分
= fit A into B
4. **sharing** [ˈʃɛrɪŋ] *a.* 共享的；共用的（動詞 share 的現在分詞作形容詞用）
share [ʃɛr] *vt.* 分享；共用

5. **service** [ˈsɜvɪs] *n.* 服務
6. **respected** [rɪˈspɛktɪd] *a.* 有聲望的，受尊敬的
7. **system** [ˈsɪstəm] *n.* 系統；制度
8. **rent** [rɛnt] *vt.* 租借
9. **quality** [ˈkwɑlətɪ] *n.* 品質

📖 閱讀理解

　　Joining a gym can be expensive, but there are ways to get fit in our own homes. One such way is by an exercise called planking. This is a great way to help your shoulders, back, stomach, hips, and bottom become stronger. In fact, planking can be good for almost every part of your body. It can even help decrease back pain. However, it is very important to plank correctly so that you do not hurt yourself. First, you need to lie face down on the ground. Then, you raise yourself up so your lower arms are on the floor and your hands are in front of your face. Your back should be straight, and your legs should be raised off the ground with the help of your toes. The idea is to hold this position for as long as possible. Over time, you should be able to hold it for longer and longer. You should give planking a try today!

　　加入健身房有可能很貴，不過有一些方法可以讓我們在自己家裡健身。其中之一是稱為平板支撐的運動。這是一個能讓你肩膀、背部、腹部、髖部以及臀部變強壯的好方法。事實上，平板支撐對身體幾乎每個部位都有好處。它甚至有助於減輕背痛。然而正確地做平板支撐是非常重要的，才不會傷到自己。首先，你必須面朝下趴在地上。然後身體向上抬起，前臂平貼地板，雙手在臉部的下前方。背部打直，以腳趾撐住離地的雙腿。運動的目的就是盡量保持這個姿勢越久越好。慢慢地，你應該能夠越撐越久。你現在就該來試試平板支撐！

<u>A</u> **1.** What is the main idea of the article?

    A. How and why to plank correctly

    B. How planking became so famous

    C. Why gyms are great places to work out

    D. Why exercise is important for our bodies

本文的主旨為何？

A. 如何與為何要正確地做平板支撐

B. 平板支撐如何變得如此出名

C. 健身房為什麼是運動的好地方

D. 運動為什麼對身體很重要

理由

問題類型：主旨題

本文前半段說明平板支撐是不用去健身房就可以在自家做的運動並對身體有許多好處，後半段則提及為何要正確地進行平板支撐運動及其正確姿勢，故得知 A 項應為正選。

<u>D</u> **2.** Which of the following pictures shows the correct way to plank, according to the article?

根據本文，下列哪一張圖顯示做平板支撐運動的正確方式？

A.

B.

C.

D.

理由

問題類型：細節題（圖片題）

根據本文第七至九句 "First, you need to lie face down on the ground. Then, you raise yourself up so your lower arms are on the floor and your hands are in front of your face. Your back should be straight, and your legs should be raised off the ground with the help of your toes."（首先，你必須面朝下趴在地上。然後身體向上抬起，前臂平貼地板，雙手在臉部的下前方。背部打直，以腳趾撐住離地的雙腿。），得知 D 項應為正選。

A 3. How does the writer finish the article?

A. By encouraging people to plank

B. By giving the history of planking

C. By listing other popular exercises

D. By discussing the advantages of walking

作者如何給本文做結尾？

A. 鼓勵大家做平板支撐

B. 介紹平板支撐運動的歷史

C. 列出其他受歡迎的運動

D. 討論步行的好處

理由

問題類型：細節題

根據本文最後一句 "You should give planking a try today!"（你現在就該來試試平板支撐！），得知 A 項應為正選。

重要單字片語

1. **planking** [ˋplæŋkɪŋ] *n.* 平板支撐；棒式運動（不可數）
   plank [plæŋk] *vi.* 做平板支撐

2. **hip** [hɪp] *n.* 髖部；臀部（常用複數）

3. **in fact** 事實上

4. **decrease** [dɪˋkris] *vt. & vi.*（使）減少（是 increase 的反義詞）

5. **raise oneself (up)** （某人）抬高身體

6. **position** [pəˋzɪʃən] *n.* 姿勢；位置

7. **over time** 漸漸地，慢慢地

8. **give sth a try** 試試看某事物
   = give sth a shot

9. **work out** 運動，健身

Unit 3 **Travel** 旅遊

段落填空

Ireland is a country in western Europe. Its main city is called Dublin. Dublin is always busy, but if you visit in the middle of March, it is __(1)__ busier than usual. __(2)__ On this day, people fill the streets and have parties. They wear green clothes, __(3)__ the color is closely linked with Ireland. They dance and sing traditional Irish songs, and they drink Guinness, which is a black beer that comes from Dublin. All of this is done __(4)__ St. Patrick, who was an important person in the Church of Ireland. The day is also celebrated all over the world, especially in the US.

CH
1

愛爾蘭是一個西歐國家。其主要城市名為都柏林。都柏林永遠都很熱鬧,但如果你在三月中旬造訪,它會比平常更加熱鬧。因為三月十七日是聖派翠克節。在這一天,人們湧向街頭,到處開著派對。他們會穿上綠色的衣服,因為綠色和愛爾蘭關係密切。大家跳著舞,唱著愛爾蘭傳統歌謠,並喝著源自於都柏林的健力士黑啤酒。這一切都是為了紀念聖派翠克,他曾是愛爾蘭教會的重要人物。世界各地也都慶祝這個日子,特別是在美國。

<u>A</u> **1.**

ⓐ 本題測試修飾形容詞或副詞比較級的副詞或詞組,主要有 much、far、even、still、a lot 等,通常置於被修飾的形容詞或副詞之前。

ⓑ 空格後為形容詞比較級 busier(較繁忙的),根據上述,A 項應為正選。

<u>B</u> **2.**

ⓐ A. The reason for this is not fully understood.
　　沒有人完全了解其原因。

　B. That is because March 17th is St. Patrick's Day.
　　這是因為三月十七日是聖派翠克節。

　C. This is mainly true in the first half of the month.
　　在這個月的上半月,這一點非常真確。

　D. There is a lot of bad weather at this time of year.
　　每年的這個時候天氣經常很差。

ⓑ 後一句敘述 "On this day, people fill the streets and have parties. They wear green clothes..."(在這一天,人們湧向街頭,到處開著派對。他們會穿上綠色的衣服……),得知本句提及某個日子,故 B 項應為正選。

11

<u>D</u> **3.**

ⓐ 本句前半句提及 "They wear green clothes"（他們會穿上綠色的衣服），後半句提及 "the color is closely linked with Ireland"（綠色和愛爾蘭關係密切），得知後半句為解釋前半句的原因，兩句須以連接詞連接。

ⓑ 根據上述，A. if（如果）、B. though（雖然）及 C. once（一旦）置入空格後語意不符，D. as（因為）符合前後文語意，故為正選。

<u>C</u> **4.**

ⓐ A. **in case of...**　萬一……

▸ In case of an earthquake, don't use the elevator.
萬一發生地震，別搭電梯。

B. **in charge of...**　負責……

▸ A new teacher will be in charge of this class this semester.
這學期會有一位新老師來管理這個班級。

C. **in memory of...**　紀念……

▸ This park was built in memory of the heroes in that war.
建造這座公園是為了紀念那場戰爭中的英雄。

D. **in favor of...**　贊成／支持……

▸ Most citizens were in favor of the idea of building a new bridge.
大部分的市民都贊成蓋一座新橋的想法。

ⓑ 根據上述，C 項應為正選。

🏷 **重要單字片語**

1. **main** [men] *a.* 主要的
   mainly [ˈmenlɪ] *adv.* 主要；通常

2. **link** [lɪŋk] *vt.* 使相關聯；連結
   be linked with / to...　與……有關聯

3. **closely** [ˈkloslɪ] *adv.* 密切地；仔細地

4. **traditional** [trəˈdɪʃənḷ] *a.* 傳統的

5. **celebrate** [ˈsɛləˌbret] *vt.* 慶祝

6. **especially** [əˈspɛʃəlɪ] *adv.* 特別地；專門地
   = particularly
   = in particular

📖 閱讀理解

The national flower of Japan is the cherry blossom. The appearance of these beautiful pink and white flowers used to tell farmers when to plant their vegetables. Now, the flowers mean hope, life, and spring to the Japanese. Citizens of the country even have parties and picnics under cherry blossom trees when the flowers are about to appear. Visitors, too, travel to Japan in April just to see the beautiful flowers. However, in 2021, the flowers arrived in March. In fact, in the city of Kyoto, they appeared earlier than at any time since the 15th century. Experts say that this is because of climate change. This is the heating of the planet that is blamed on human activity. Warmer temperatures mean that spring arrives earlier and the flowers come out earlier. They also mean that visitors wishing to see Japan's cherry blossoms might need to book an earlier trip in the future.

日本的國花是櫻花。這些美麗的粉紅及白色花朵的初放時刻曾被用來提醒農民何時該種植蔬菜。現在櫻花對日本人來說代表希望、生命與春天。該國人民甚至會在櫻花即將盛開時，在櫻花樹下舉辦派對和野餐。遊客也會在四月時來日本一遊只為賞花。然而在 2021 年，櫻花在三月便來報到。事實上，在京都市，櫻花出現的時間比十五世紀以來任何一次花期都早。專家說這是因為氣候變遷，亦即人類活動導致的地球暖化。較高的氣溫代表春天提早到來，花朵也較早綻放。這也意味著想一睹日本櫻花的遊客，未來可能得預訂時間提前的旅遊行程。

D 1. What is the main focus of the article?
　　A. The loss of a highly popular tree
　　B. The warm summer weather in Japan
　　C. The reasons for the picnic habit in Japan
　　D. The early appearance of a famous flower

本文主要的重點是什麼？
A. 一種廣受喜愛的樹種消失
B. 日本夏季的溫暖天候
C. 日本習於野餐的原因
D. 一種知名花種提早開花

理由

問題類型： 主旨題
本文前半部介紹日本的櫻花對日本人的意義及盛開時節當地人會從事的活動，後半部提及 2021 年櫻花提早開花的情形，故 D 項應為正選。

C **2.** According to the article, why do visitors go to Japan in the spring?
A. To help out on farms
B. To learn about Kyoto
C. To look at beautiful views
D. To enjoy the cool weather

根據本文，遊客為什麼在春天時造訪日本？
A. 協助農事
B. 了解京都
C. 觀賞美麗的風景
D. 享受涼爽的天氣

理由

問題類型：細節題

根據本文第五句 "Visitors, too, travel to Japan in April just to see the beautiful flowers." （遊客也會在四月時來日本一遊只為賞花。），得知 C 項應為正選。

B **3.** Which of the following is explained in this article?
A. Why a Japanese tradition disappeared
B. Why something took place in Japan in 2021
C. Why temperatures are getting colder on Earth
D. Why Japanese people changed a habit in 2021

本文解釋了下列哪一項？
A. 一項日本傳統為何消失
B. 2021 年日本為何發生了某件事
C. 地球上的氣溫為何越來越低
D. 日本人為何在 2021 年改變了一項習慣

理由

問題類型：細節題

本文第六句提及 2021 年日本櫻花提早盛開，而倒數第四至二句說明其原因為氣候變遷的關係，人類活動造成地球暖化，使得花朵提早綻放，得知 B 項應為正選。

🏷 重要單字片語

1. **cherry blossom**　　櫻花
   cherry [ˋtʃɛrɪ] *n.* 櫻桃（樹）
   blossom [ˋblɑsəm] *n.* （果樹的）花

2. **appearance** [əˋpɪrəns] *n.* （首次）出現；外表
   appear [əˋpɪr] *vi.* 出現
   = show up
   disappear [ˏdɪsəˋpɪr] *vi.* 消失

3. **used to V**　　過去曾做……；過去習慣做……

4. **expert** [ˋɛkspɚt] *n.* 專家

5. **climate** [ˋklaɪmɪt] *n.* 氣候（指某地長期的氣象型態）
   比較：
   weather [ˋwɛðɚ] *n.* 天氣（指某地短期的氣象型態，不可數）

6. **planet** [ˋplænɪt] *n.* 行星，星球
   比較：
   star [stɑr] *n.* 恆星

7. **be blamed on...**　　是……的原因；被歸咎於……

8. **focus** [ˋfokəs] *n.* 焦點

9. **help out**　　協助

Unit 4 News Reports 新聞報導

三 段落填空

Tatler is the name of a famous British magazine. It is also printed with different articles in Taiwan and other Asian countries. In 2021, many of the writers chose their favorite cities for food in Asia. __(1)__ That is because the food in Taipei is of good quality and is easy to find. *Tatler*'s article __(2)__ the city for its mix of local, national, and international food. It also __(3)__ several places for special praise. These include the large fish market in Zhongshan, the tea restaurants in Maokong, and the dumplings at Din Tai Fung. And of course, no discussion of Taipei's food would be complete __(4)__ the traditional night markets.

Tatler 是一本英國知名雜誌的名稱。它在臺灣和其他亞洲國家發行的版本會有不同的報導文章。2021 年時，許多該雜誌的作家選出他們最喜歡的亞洲美食之都。除了東京、首爾及其他城市之外，臺北也名列此名單中。那是因為臺北的食物品質好又不難找。Tatler 的報導稱讚臺北結合了在地的、全國性的和國際的美食。它還挑出幾個地點來特別稱讚一番。其中包括中山區的大型魚市、貓空的茶餐廳和鼎泰豐的小籠包。當然，任何關於臺北美食的討論若沒包含傳統夜市就不算完整。

__D__ **1.**

ⓐ A. The article can also be viewed on the internet.
這篇文章也可以在網路上閱覽。

B. Sadly, they rated Taipei's food as lacking in taste.
可惜的是，他們認為臺北的食物欠缺品味。

C. All of them agreed that Bangkok was by far the best.
他們一致認為曼谷遙遙領先。

D. Along with Tokyo, Seoul, and others, Taipei was on this list.
除了東京、首爾及其他城市之外，臺北也名列此名單中。

ⓑ 根據空格前一句 "In 2021, many of the writers chose their favorite cities for food in Asia."（2021 年時，許多該雜誌的作家選出他們最喜歡的亞洲美食之都。）及空格後一句 "That is because the food in Taipei is of good quality and is easy to find."（那是因為臺北的食物品質好又不難找。），可推知臺北也是上述亞洲美食之都之一，且 D 項置入空格後符合上下文語意，故應為正選。

<u>C</u> **2.**

ⓐ A. **direct** [dəˈrɛkt] *vt.* 給……指引方向

  direct sb to + 地方　　指引某人到某地

  ▸ Could you direct me to the campus bookstore?
  你可以告訴我怎麼去校園書店嗎？

 B. **provide** [prəˈvaɪd] *vt.* 提供

  provide sb with sth　　提供某物給某人

 = provide sth for sb

  ▸ Jack provided his mother with enough money to buy a new house.
  傑克給他母親足夠買一棟新房子的錢。

 C. **admire** [ədˈmaɪr] *vt.* 欽佩，讚賞

  admire sb/sth for + N/V-ing　　欽佩某人 / 物……

  ▸ We admire Amy for her ability, but we don't particularly like her.
  我們欽佩艾咪的能力，但並不特別喜歡她。

 D. **require** [rɪˈkwaɪr] *vt.* 需要；要求

  ▸ Most house plants require regular watering.
  大部分室內盆栽需要定期澆水。

ⓑ 根據上述，C 項應為正選。

<u>A</u> **3.**

ⓐ A. **pick out...**　　挑選……

  ▸ Mary picked out a gift for her mother's birthday.
  瑪麗為她媽媽的生日挑選了一份禮物。

 B. **care for...**　　照顧……

 = look after...

  ▸ Mariah has been caring for her mother since her father died.
  自從瑪麗亞的爸爸去世後，她就一直照顧媽媽。

 C. **leave out...**　　漏掉……

  ▸ Don't leave out any details when you tell me about your date last night.
  你在跟我說你昨晚約會的事時，可別漏掉任何小細節。

 D. **figure out...**　　想出 / 理解……

  ▸ We were unable to figure out the answer to the question.
  我們想不出這問題的答案。

ⓑ 根據上述，A 項應為正選。

CH
1

D **4.**

ⓐ A. including 為介詞，後接名詞作前述事項的補充說明，前面通常要加一逗點。

▶ All the students, including Andy, will go to the picnic.

所有學生，包括安迪，都會去野餐。

B. to include 置入空格句意不合邏輯。

C. and include 置入空格句意不合邏輯。

D. No + N + would be complete without + N/V-ing

= N + wouldn't be complete without + N/V-ing

（此處為雙重否定用法，表「若沒有……，……就不算完整」，可表肯定的意思，即「有了……，……才算完整」。）

ⓑ 根據上述，D 項應為正選。

🏷 重要單字片語

1. **local** [ˈlokl̩] *a.* 當地的，本地的

2. **international** [ˌɪntɚˈnæʃənl̩] *a.* 國際的

3. **praise** [prez] *n.* 稱讚，讚美

4. **dumpling** [ˈdʌmplɪŋ] *n.* 包餡的食品（如小籠包、水餃、湯圓等）

5. **discussion** [dɪˈskʌʃən] *n.* 討論

6. **complete** [kəmˈplit] *a.* 完整的，完全的

7. **by far + the + 形容詞最高級** 最最……的

8. **along with...** 除……之外（還有……）

📖 閱讀理解

Many people these days use their phones all the time. They even play games and send messages on their phones while they walk the streets. This can be dangerous, and some people have walked into things and hurt themselves. Paeng Min-wook, a design student from South Korea, has invented an item that could stop this from happening. It is called The Third Eye. It is a round ball that can be fixed to the center of your head, above your real eyes. When you lower your neck to check your phone, The Third Eye "opens." If it senses you are about to walk into something, an alarm goes off. However, Paeng does not really think that The Third Eye is a solution to people using their phones at the cost of their safety. Rather, he wants people to hear about The Third Eye and realize that they should put their phones down more often. He joked that if they don't, humans will need a real extra eye in the future.

現在許多人無時無刻不在用手機。他們甚至在路上邊走邊玩手機遊戲跟傳訊息。這是很危險的，還有人撞到東西受傷。韓國的設計系學生彭閔旭發明了一種防止這種事情發生的產品。它叫作「第三隻眼」。它是一顆圓球，可以安在頭中央，真正眼睛的上方。當你低頭看手機時，第三隻眼會「睜開」。如果它感應到你快要撞到東西，警鈴就會響起。然而彭閔旭並不覺得第三隻眼對那些不顧自己安全也要用手機的人而言，是個真正的解決方案。他其實是想讓大家在聽到有第三隻眼這種東西後，理解到自己應該要更常把手機放下才行。他開玩笑說，如果大家不這樣做，人類在未來會真的需要多一隻眼睛才行。

A **1.** What would be the best title for this article in a newspaper?
A. *Student Invents The Third Eye*
B. *Eye Game Becomes Popular*
C. *The Third Eye Operation Successful*
D. *Student Hurt While Using Phone*

這篇報紙報導的最佳標題會是什麼？
A. 學生發明第三隻眼
B. 眼睛遊戲流行起來
C. 第三隻眼行動成功
D. 學生用手機時受傷

理由

問題類型：**主旨題**

本文第一至三句描述許多現代人過度使用手機到可能危害自身安全的情形，第四至八句則敘述一位韓國學生發明了有助於防止這種狀況發生的「第三隻眼」，以及第三隻眼如何運作，故 A 項應為正選。

D **2.** Which picture correctly shows the style and position of The Third Eye?
哪一張圖正確顯示第三隻眼的造型和安裝位置？

A.
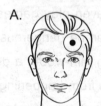

B.
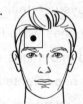

C.

D.

理由

問題類型： 細節題（圖片題）

根據本文第六句 "It is a round ball that can be fixed to the center of your head, above your real eyes."（它是一顆圓球，可以安在頭中央，真正眼睛的上方。），得知 D 項應為正選。

A **3.** What does Paeng want to achieve?

A. People using their phones less

B. An increase in jokes about eyes

C. An increase in the cost of phones

D. Millions of sales of The Third Eye

彭閔旭想要達到什麼目標？

A. 大家少用手機

B. 增加有關眼睛的笑話

C. 提高手機的價格

D. 賣出好幾百萬個第三隻眼

理由

問題類型： 推論題

根據本文倒數第二句 "Rather, he wants people to hear about The Third Eye and realize that they should put their phones down more often."（他其實是想讓大家在聽到有第三隻眼這種東西後，理解到自己應該要更常把手機放下才行。），得知 A 項應為正選。

重要單字片語

1. **walk into sth** 走路時撞上某物

2. **lower** [ˈloɚ] vt. 低下，降低

3. **sense** [sɛns] vt. 感應到，測出

4. **alarm** [əˈlɑrm] n. 警報器

5. **go off** （信號、警報器）響起

6. **solution** [səˈluʃən] n. 解決辦法（與介詞 to 並用）

   a solution to... ……的解決辦法

7. **at the cost of...** 犧牲……，以……的代價

8. **operation** [ˌɑpəˈreʃən] n. 行動；運作；手術

9. **achieve** [əˈtʃiv] vt. 達到，完成（目標、任務等）

Family 家庭

段落填空

Who makes the meals in your family? Perhaps it's your mom, who gets home from the office before anyone else. Perhaps it's your dad, who no longer works. Maybe you even do the cooking yourself. If you want to give the cook a __(1)__ , though, you could always ask a robot to do it. A company __(2)__ Moley Robotics has created a "robot kitchen." The robot can take items from the refrigerator, use the range and the kitchen sink, and serve dishes. It can even do the washing-up. __(3)__ This high price means you might have to __(4)__ your mom and dad's cooking for a while longer.

你家是誰在做飯？也許是下班後比別人早回到家的媽媽。也許是你那已不再上班的爸爸。甚至可能是你自己下廚。不過如果你想讓做飯的人休息一下，總是可以找機器人代勞。一家名為莫利機器人的公司創造了一間「機器人廚房」。裡頭的機器人會開冰箱拿東西、使用爐灶和廚房水槽，還會上菜。它甚至還會洗碗。但是這個機器人要價約臺幣一千萬元。這個天價意味著你可能得再忍受你父母的廚藝好一段時間。

B **1.**

ⓐ A. **limit** [`ˋlɪmɪt] *n.* 限制；極限

▶ The speed limit is 100 kilometers per hour on this road.
這條路的速限是時速一百公里。

＊ **per** [pɝ] / [pɚ] *prep.* 每……

B. **break** [brek] *n.* 休息

take a break　休息一下

give sb a break　讓某人休息一下；饒了某人

▶ After the class exercised for thirty minutes, the teacher gave them a break.
全班運動三十分鐘後，老師讓大家休息一下。

C. **mark** [mɑrk] *n.* 分數；記號

▶ The teacher gave Nadia extra marks for her efforts.
老師因為娜迪亞很認真而給她加分。

D. **reason** [`ˋrizn̩] *n.* 理由（可數）；理性（不可數）

▶ There's no reason for me to reject Tony's offer to help.
我沒有理由拒絕湯尼要幫忙的好意。

ⓑ 根據上述，B 項應為正選。

__C__ **2.**

ⓐ 原句實為：

A company <u>which is called</u> Moley Robotics has created a "robot kitchen."

限定修飾的形容詞子句（即關係代名詞之前無逗點）中，若關係代名詞作主詞，該形容詞子句

可依下列步驟簡化為分詞片語，步驟如下：

(1) 刪除關係代名詞；

(2) 後面的動詞改為現在分詞（若動詞為 be 動詞，則改為現在分詞 being 後可予省略）。

ⓑ 根據上述，which is called 可改為 called，故 C 項應為正選。

__D__ **3.**

ⓐ A. It turns itself off when finished.

當它完成工作時會自動關機。

B. What it can't do is buy the food.

它不會做的事是採買食物。

C. However, the meals don't taste good.

然而那些餐點不太好吃。

D. However, it costs around NT$10 million.

但是這個機器人要價約臺幣一千萬元。

ⓑ 後句主詞為 This high price（這個天價），得知本句應提及價錢，故 D 項應為正選。

__A__ **4.**

ⓐ A. **put up with...**　　忍受……

▶ Mina couldn't put up with her boyfriend's bad temper any more.

米娜再也無法忍受她男友的壞脾氣了。

B. **run out of...**　　用完……

▶ We've run out of salt. Would you get some in the supermarket?

我們的鹽用完了。你可以去超市買一點嗎？

C. **take care of...**　　照顧……

▶ Phoebe took care of her grandma after her grandpa passed away.

菲碧的祖父過世後便由她照顧祖母。

D. **do away with sth**　　丟棄／擺脫／廢除某事物

▶ Let's do away with all these empty beer bottles.

我們把這些空啤酒瓶都丟掉吧。

ⓑ 根據上述，A 項應為正選。

🏷️ **重要單字片語**

1. **no longer**　不再
 = not... any more
2. **robot** [ˈrobət] *n.* 機器人
3. **item** [ˈaɪtəm] *n.* 物品
4. **refrigerator** [rɪˈfrɪdʒəˌretɚ] *n.* 冰箱
 (= fridge [frɪdʒ])
5. **range** [rendʒ] *n.* 爐灶；範圍
6. **sink** [sɪŋk] *n.*（廚房內的）水槽
7. **washing-up** [ˈwɑʃɪŋˌʌp] *n.* 清洗餐具
 （不可數）
8. **turn off... / turn... off**　關掉……的電源

📖 **閱讀理解**

When you think of the word "family," you probably think of your parents and brothers or sisters. That is, you think of human families. However, animals have families, too. And just like in human families, the older members give the younger members advice and help. Take sperm whales, for example. These large sea animals were often hunted and killed during the 19th century. However, a study by The Royal Society shows that the whales learned how to avoid the hunters' weapons. The older, more experienced whales then taught the younger ones where to swim to get away from the hunters. The hunters were therefore able to kill far fewer whales. Very few countries now support the killing of whales. These clever animals, therefore, may now be able to pass on different information to their families. Scientists hope that whales can learn the positions of all the trash in the oceans. If the older whales can teach the younger ones how to avoid this trash, more families of whales will be saved.

當你想到「家庭」這個字時，可能想到的是你的父母和兄弟姊妹。也就是說，你想到的是人類的家庭。但動物也有家庭。就如同人類的家庭一般，動物家庭中年長的成員會給幼小的成員建議和協助。以抹香鯨為例。這些大型海洋動物在十九世紀間經常被獵捕及殺害。不過一項由皇家學會所做的研究顯示，這些鯨魚學會了如何避開捕鯨人的獵具。然後較年長且較有經驗的鯨魚會教導幼鯨在遠離捕鯨人的地帶巡游。因此捕鯨人殺死的鯨魚數量便大幅減少。現在只有極少數的國家支持捕殺鯨魚。因此這些聰明的動物現在可以將不同的訊息傳達給家庭成員。科學家希望鯨魚能知道海洋中所有垃圾的位置。如果年長鯨魚能教導幼鯨如何避開這些垃圾，更多的鯨魚家族將因而得救。

__C__ **1.** Which of the following is the primary focus of this article?

　　A. A study into small sea animals

　　B. An animal that no longer exists today

　　C. An animal that learned to avoid danger

　　D. A family of hunters in the 19th century

下列哪一項是本文的要點？

A. 一項對小型海洋動物的研究

B. 一種現已不復存在的動物

C. 一種學會避開危險的動物

D. 十九世紀的一個狩獵家族

> 理由

問題類型：__主旨題__

本文第一至四句敘述人類及動物「家庭」的共同點，第五至最後一句說明抹香鯨家族內年長鯨魚指導幼鯨規避危險的特性，得知 C 項應為正選。

__D__ **2.** What did the older whales do when they were hunted?

　　A. They swam away from their families.

　　B. They asked the younger whales for help.

　　C. They gave up and were caught by the hunters.

　　D. They passed on knowledge to younger whales.

在過去，年長的鯨魚被獵捕時會做什麼？

A. 牠們會遠離家族成員。

B. 牠們會求助於幼鯨。

C. 牠們會放棄抵抗，然後被捕鯨人獵捕。

D. 牠們會傳授知識給幼鯨。

> 理由

問題類型：__細節題__

根據本文第六句 "These large sea animals were often hunted and killed during the 19th century."（這些大型的海洋動物在十九世紀間經常被獵捕及殺害。）及第八句 "The older, more experienced whales then taught the younger ones where to swim to get away from the hunters."（然後較年長且較有經驗的鯨魚會教導幼鯨在遠離捕鯨人的地帶巡游。），得知 D 項應為正選。

__D__ **3.** What do scientists hope whales will do today?

　　A. Stop leaving their families

　　B. Help to clean up the oceans

　　C. Teach other animals fun tricks

　　D. Learn how to keep away from garbage

現在的科學家希望鯨魚做什麼？

A. 不要再離開牠們的家族

B. 協助清潔海洋

C. 教導其他動物好玩的特技

D. 學習如何遠離垃圾

> 理由

問題類型：__細節題__

根據本文倒數兩句 "Scientists hope that whales can learn the positions of all the trash in the oceans. If the older whales can teach the younger ones how to avoid this trash, more families of whales will be saved."（科學家希望鯨魚能知道海洋中所有垃圾的位置。如果年長鯨魚能教導幼鯨如何避開這些垃圾，更多的鯨魚家族將因而得救。），得知 D 項應為正選。

重要單字片語

1. **advice** [əd`vaɪs] *n.* 建議，忠告，勸告（不可數）
   a piece of advice　　一則忠告，一個建議

2. **take..., for example**　　以……為例

3. **a sperm whale**　　抹香鯨

4. **weapon** [`wɛpən] *n.* 武器

5. **get away from...**　　遠離……
   = keep away from...

6. **clever** [`klɛvɚ] *a.* 聰明的

7. **pass on sth / pass sth on**
   傳遞某事物

8. **position** [pə`zɪʃən] *n.* 位置；地位；職務

9. **exist** [ɪg`zɪst] *vi.* 存在

10. **give up (...) / gave (...) up**
    放棄（……）

Unit 6 Entertainment 娛樂

三 段落填空

If you were asked to name a famous Taiwanese movie director, you would probably say Ang Lee. He has made great films __(1)__ *Brokeback Mountain* and *Life of Pi*. __(2)__ One such director was Edward Yang. Yang was brought up in Taipei and then traveled to the US to study. When he realized that he wanted to make films, he came back to Taiwan. Most of his movies are set in cities. They deal with __(3)__ like the conflict between the traditional and modern worlds. Perhaps his most famous film is *Yi Yi*, __(4)__ about a middle-class family in Taipei. It won lots of major prizes.

如果要你說出一位知名臺灣電影導演的名字，你可能會說李安。他拍過像是《斷背山》和《少年 Pi 的奇幻漂流》等佳片。不過，臺灣還有許多其他成功的導演。其中一位是楊德昌。楊德昌在臺北長大，後來去美國留學。他發現自己想拍電影，於是回到臺灣。他大部分的電影都以都市為背景。這些電影探討像是傳統與現代社會間衝突這類的話題。他最著名的電影可能是《一一》，故事圍繞著一個臺北市的中產階級家庭打轉。該片贏得過許多大獎。

D **1.**

ⓐ A. **along with...**　　連同……（一起）

= together with...

▶ Jack, along with his manager, took part in the meeting.
傑克和他的經理一起參與了該場會議。

B. **thanks to...**　　多虧／由於……

▶ Thanks to Albert's help, I was able to finish the work on time.
多虧艾伯特的幫助，我才能準時把工作做完。

C. **rather than...**　　而非……

Rather than + V/V-ing, S + V　　不做……而做……

▶ Rather than playing pool, we went bowling.
我們沒去打撞球而去打保齡球。

D. **such as...**　　像是／諸如……

▶ John has many hobbies, such as jogging, hiking, and stamp collecting.
約翰有多種嗜好，像是慢跑、健行、集郵等。

ⓑ 根據語意，得知 D 項應為正選。

CH
1

<u>B</u> **2.**

ⓐ A. In fact, the history of Taiwanese movies can be traced back to 1901.
事實上，臺灣電影的歷史可追溯至 1901 年。

B. However, there have been many other successful directors from Taiwan.
不過，臺灣還有許多其他成功的導演。

C. On the other hand, the director has spent most of his adult life in the US.
另一方面，該導演成年後的大部分時間都在美國度過。

D. At the time of this writing, Ang Lee has directed fourteen successful movies.
在撰寫本文時，李安已經執導了十四部成功的電影。

ⓑ 前兩句提及李安是知名的臺灣電影導演且拍攝過多部好電影，且根據空格後一句 "One such director was Edward Yang."（其中一位是楊德昌。），得知 B 項置入空格後符合上下文語意，故應為正選。

<u>A</u> **3.**

ⓐ A. **topic** [ˈtɑpɪk] *n.* 主題
　▸ The article covered a wide range of topics.
　這篇文章討論了範圍很廣的許多主題。

B. **opinion** [əˈpɪnjən] *n.* 意見
　▸ In my opinion, we shouldn't allow Gary to do the job.
　依我之見，我們不該讓蓋瑞做這項工作。

C. **project** [ˈprɑdʒɛkt] *n.* 計畫；專案
　▸ The project to put a man on the moon succeeded in 1969.
　送人類登陸月球的計畫在 1969 年實現了。

D. **memory** [ˈmɛmərɪ] *n.* 回憶（常用複數）；記性
　▸ These photos bring back lots of sad memories.
　這些照片喚起了許多令人傷心的回憶。

ⓑ 根據上述，A 項應為正選。

<u>C</u> **4.**

ⓐ 空格前為完整句子 "Perhaps his most famous film is *Yi Yi*, ..."（他最著名的電影可能是《一一》，……），空格後為介詞 about（關於）及名詞詞組 a middle-class family in Taipei（一個臺北市的中產階級家庭），得知此處須置關係代名詞 which / that 及 be 動詞，which / that 引導形容詞子句修飾前面的名詞 *Yi Yi*。惟形容詞子句前<u>若有逗點</u>，關係代名詞不可用 <u>that</u>。

ⓑ 根據上述，C 項應為正選。

重要單字片語

1. **name** [nem] *vt.* 說出……的名字／名稱 & *n.* 名字

2. **director** [dəˋrɛktɚ] *n.* 導演

3. **bring up sb / bring sb up**　養育某人

4. **be set in...**　（小說、電影）以……為背景

5. **deal with sth**　探討／論述某事物

6. **conflict** [ˋkɑnflɪkt] *n.* 衝突；抵觸
   the conflict between A and B
   A 與 B 之間的衝突

7. **middle-class** [ˋmɪdḷˋklæs] *a.* 中產階級的
   the middle class　中產階級

8. **be traced (back) to...**　追溯到……

9. **successful** [səkˋsɛsfəl] *a.* 成功的

10. **on the other hand**　另一方面（常與 on the one hand（一方面）並用）

閱讀理解

Children across the world have enjoyed reading stories about Paddington Bear for over sixty years. A British writer named Michael Bond created the character in the late 1950s. Paddington is a talking bear. He wears an old hat and a thick coat and carries a travel bag. In his first story, he is found at London Paddington train station by a family called the Browns. He goes to live with the family and has lots of fun times. He is a very kind bear, but he often gets into trouble and has to work hard to get out of it. Kids love the stories about Paddington Bear because he is cute and funny. Adults can safely read the stories to their children because good always beats evil. There are other ways to experience the stories, too. There are several television shows about Paddington Bear. There are some successful movies as well. And there is a lot of information about the character at the Museum of London.

六十多年來，全世界的小孩都喜歡閱讀帕丁頓熊的故事。英國作家邁克・龐德在五〇年代末創造了這個角色。帕丁頓熊是一隻會說話的熊。他戴著一頂舊帽子、穿著一件厚外套，手上還拎著一個旅行包。在他的第一則故事中，他在倫敦帕丁頓火車站被名叫布朗的一家人發現。他接下來就跟著那家人住，而且過得很開心。他是一隻非常體貼善良的熊，但經常惹麻煩，而且必須很辛苦才能脫困。小朋友很喜歡帕丁頓熊的故事，因為他既萌又有趣。大人可以放心讀這些故事給孩子聽，因為最後總是邪不勝正。還有其他方式可以體驗這些故事。有幾檔帕丁頓熊的電視節目。也有一些賣座電影。倫敦博物館也有很多關於這個角色的資訊。

C 1. Based on the article, what does Paddington Bear look like?

根據本文,帕丁頓熊的樣貌為何?

A.

B.

C.

D.

理由

問題類型: 細節題(圖片題)

根據本文第四句 "He wears an old hat and a thick coat and carries a travel bag."(他戴著一頂舊帽子、穿著一件厚外套,手上還拎著一個旅行包。),得知 C 項應為正選。

A 2. What is NOT true about Paddington Bear?

A. His story is based on the life of a train driver.

B. Children can learn good things from his stories.

C. Children like him because he makes them laugh.

D. He is a bear that always thinks about others' feelings.

關於帕丁頓熊,哪一項敘述不正確?

A. 他的故事是根據一名火車司機的一生改編的。

B. 孩子們可以從他的故事中學到好的事情。

C. 孩子們喜歡他,因為他讓他們開懷大笑。

D. 他是隻總是會顧慮別人感受的熊。

理由

問題類型: 細節題

根據本文第二句 "A British writer named Michael Bond created the character in the late 1950s."(英國作家邁克·龐德在五〇年代末創造了這個角色。),得知 A 項敘述不正確,故應為正選。

A 3. Which way of enjoying the Paddington Bear stories does the article focus on?

本文聚焦於哪一種欣賞帕丁頓熊故事的方式？

A. The books
B. The movies
C. The museum
D. The TV shows

A. 書本
B. 電影
C. 博物館
D. 電視節目

CH 1

理由

問題類型：細節題

根據本文第一句 "Children across the world have enjoyed reading stories about Paddington Bear for over sixty years."（六十多年來，全世界的小孩都喜歡閱讀帕丁頓熊的故事。）及倒數第五句 "Adults can safely read the stories to their children because good always beats evil."（大人可以放心讀這些故事給孩子聽，因為最後總是邪不勝正。），可推知閱讀帕丁頓熊的故事書是多年來孩童欣賞其故事的主要管道，故 A 項應為正選。

🏷 重要單字片語

1. **create** [krɪˈet] *vt.* 創造，創作
2. **get into trouble**　惹上麻煩，陷入困境
3. **get out of...**　擺脫 / 逃離……
4. **beat** [bit] *vt.* 戰勝，擊敗

5. **evil** [ˈivḷ] *n.* 邪惡（之事）；罪惡（行為）& *a.* 邪惡的
6. **as well**　也（= too，置句尾）
7. **museum** [mjuˈzɪəm] *n.* 博物館
8. **(be) based on...**　根據……

School & Education 學校與教育

段落填空

Starting school can be exciting for young children. It provides a chance to be in a different environment and learn new things. However, for some, starting school for the first time can be hard. They may feel __(1)__ about being away from their parents. They may worry about meeting new children and making new friends. __(2)__ Moms and dads can find __(3)__ hard to leave their children in the care of someone else. It might be the first time they have had to do this. Starting school, __(4)__, is a natural part of life. It is the beginning of a fun, new chapter in the lives of children and their parents.

開始上學對幼童來說可能很令人興奮。學校給他們在不同環境中學習新事物的機會。然而對某些孩子來說,第一次上學可能相當掙扎。他們對於離開父母身邊可能會感到緊張,也可能對認識其他小孩以及結交新朋友感到擔心。這對父母來說也許同樣很煎熬。爸媽們可能會覺得很難把小孩交給別人來照顧。這可能是他們第一次得這樣做。儘管如此,開始上學是人生必經的過程。它是兒童與父母的人生中一個有趣且嶄新的階段。

__B__ **1.**

ⓐ A. **tired** [taɪrd] *a.* 感到疲倦的;感到厭煩的
  ▶ Mike was so tired that he couldn't focus on anything today.
    麥克今天很累,做什麼事都無法專注。

  B. **nervous** [ˋnɝvəs] *a.* 緊張的
  ▶ Andy got very nervous before meeting his girlfriend's parents.
    安迪在會見他女友的父母前非常緊張。

  C. **lucky** [ˋlʌkɪ] *a.* 幸運的
  ▶ Heidi felt lucky to have such a good family.
    海蒂覺得擁有這麼好的家庭很幸運。

  D. **excited** [ɪkˋsaɪtɪd] *a.* 感到興奮的
    be / get excited about...   對……感到興奮
  ▶ All the students were very excited about the graduation trip.
    這些學生都對畢業旅行感到興奮不已。

ⓑ 根據上述,**B** 項應為正選。

<u>D</u> **2.**

ⓐ A. There are ways to make this simpler.
有些方法可以讓這件事變簡單。

B. The teachers can help during this time.
在這段時間裡，老師可以幫忙。

C. On the other hand, parents find it easy.
另一方面，父母親覺得這很容易。

D. It can also be a difficult time for parents.
這對父母來說也許同樣很煎熬。

ⓑ 空格前三句提及某些孩子第一次上學會感到緊張和擔憂，而空格後句敘述父母對於把小孩交給
另一個人來照顧可能也會覺得很掙扎，D 項置入空格後符合前後文語意，故應為正選。

<u>C</u> **3.**

ⓐ 本題測試下列句型中 it 當虛受詞的用法：

find it + Adj. + to V　　覺得做……很……

▸ Robert found it difficult to ask others for help.
羅伯特覺得開口向別人求助很困難。

ⓑ 根據上述，C 項應為正選。

<u>A</u> **4.**

ⓐ A. **though** [ðo] *adv.* 然而，不過

▸ Benny is my cousin. We haven't seen each other for years, though.
班尼是我的表弟。但我們已經很多年沒見了。

B. **finally** [ˈfaɪnl̩ɪ] *adv.* 最後；終於（= at last）

▸ Jessie finally won first place in the speech contest.
潔西最後在演講比賽中獲得第一名。

C. **therefore** [ˈðɛrˌfɔr] *adv.* 因此

▸ I have to get up early tomorrow. Therefore, I'll go to bed now.
我明天得早起。所以我現在要上床睡覺了。

D. **especially** [əˈspɛʃəlɪ] *adv.* 尤其是，特別是

▸ Karen likes to eat Japanese food, especially ramen.
凱倫喜歡吃日本料理，尤其是拉麵。

ⓑ 根據上述，A 項應為正選。

🏷️ 重要單字片語

1. **environment** [ɪnˈvaɪrənmənt] *n.* 環境
2. **worry about...** 擔心……
3. **in the care of...** 由……照顧
4. **chapter** [ˈtʃæptɚ] *n.* 階段，時期；篇章

📖 閱讀理解

When we are at school, we are taught that certain things are true. We are told that these are facts and that they are correct. However, when more information is discovered, sometimes "facts" can change. For instance, you may have been told that the Great Wall of China can be seen from space. It used to be said that the wall was the only object made by man that was like this. People who have traveled to the moon or into space, though, say this is not true. From space, the wall just mixes into the countryside around it. Another "fact" that has changed is also to do with space. Generations of children have been told that there are nine planets. Pluto, the furthest from the sun, was said to be the ninth. Scientists, though, have discovered more information. They now consider Pluto too small to be a planet. Thus, there are just eight main planets.

　　我們在求學時，會被教導說某些事是真理。我們被告知這些是事實且千真萬確。然而當更多資訊被發現時，有時候「事實」也是會改變的。舉例來說，可能有人告訴你從外太空可以看見中國的萬里長城。以前都說長城是外太空可見的唯一人造物。但曾經登陸月球或前往外太空的人說這不是真的。從外太空看，長城是隱沒在周遭鄉野之中的。另一個已改變的「事實」也和外太空有關。許多世代的孩童都被告知太陽系的行星共有九顆。距離太陽最遠的冥王星是第九顆行星。但科學家已發現了更多資訊。他們現在認為冥王星太小不能稱之為行星。因此主要行星只有八顆。

__A__ **1.** What would be the primary purpose of reading the article?
A. To understand that facts can change
B. To encourage people to become teachers
C. To realize that traveling into space is hard
D. To learn that information always stays the same

閱讀本文的主要目的可能是哪一項？
A. 理解事實會改變
B. 鼓勵大家當老師
C. 了解外太空旅行很困難
D. 理解到資訊是永遠不會改變的

理由
問題類型：主旨題
本文第一至三句說明「事實」可能會因為新的發現而改變，而第四至最後一句列舉兩個過去被認可而今已被推翻的「事實」，得知 A 項應為正選。

CH 1

<u>C</u> **2.** Why can't the Great Wall of China be seen from space?

A. Parts of it have been moved.

B. There is too much bad weather.

C. It gets lost in the area around it.

D. The wall is shorter than we thought.

為什麼從外太空看不到中國的萬里長城？

A. 其某些部分已被搬移。

B. 太常有壞天氣。

C. 它隱藏在周遭區域中。

D. 長城比我們想像的要短。

理由

問題類型：細節題

根據本文第七句 "From space, the wall just mixes into the countryside around it."（從外太空看，長城是隱沒在周遭鄉野之中的。），得知 C 項應為正選。

<u>D</u> **3.** What does the writer suggest in the article?

A. We should try to discover facts on our own.

B. Pluto is now the furthest planet from Earth.

C. A new planet has been found in place of Pluto.

D. We shouldn't believe everything we learn at school.

作者在本文中暗示哪一項？

A. 我們應該嘗試自己發現事實。

B. 冥王星現在是距離地球最遠的行星。

C. 已找到一顆取代冥王星的新行星。

D. 我們不能相信在學校裡所學的一切。

理由

問題類型：推論題

本文第一至三句敘述某些過去習得的知識會因為新的發現而改變，而後文列舉了中國的萬里長城及冥王星的例子，得知學校裡所學的知識並非永遠為真，故 D 項應為正選。

重要單字片語

1. **certain** [ˋsɝtn̩] *a.* 某些（= some）
2. **discover** [dɪsˋkʌvɚ] *vt.* 發現
3. **object** [ˋɑbdʒɪkt] *n.* 物體
4. **countryside** [ˋkʌntrɪˏsaɪd] *n.* 鄉間（不可數）
   the countryside　鄉下；郊外
   = the country

5. **generation** [ˏdʒɛnəˋreʃən] *n.* 世代
6. **in place of...**　取代……

Shopping 購物

段落填空

Some people love shopping; others hate it. But we all have to do it, __(1)__ it's buying food, clothes, or even other less important items. When the world was hit by COVID-19, many people were unable to shop in traditional stores. Rather, they had to buy their goods on the internet. Millions of people, especially in the west, have continued to use Amazon for this __(2)__ for years. It is available in over fifty countries. Although Amazon can ship some goods to Taiwan, there is no Amazon Taiwan. Therefore, __(3)__ to buy things on the internet. These and many other companies saw their orders __(4)__ quickly in Taiwan during COVID-19.

有些人喜歡購物，有些人則很討厭。但我們總得買東西，不管是食物、衣服，甚至是其他較不重要的物品。全世界受到新冠肺炎襲擊後，許多人無法在傳統商店購物，而得在網路上購買商品。數以百萬計的人，尤其是西方人，已經為此目的持續光顧亞馬遜網站多年。亞馬遜在五十多個國家架設專用網站。雖然亞馬遜可以將某些商品運到臺灣，不過並沒有亞馬遜臺灣區網站。因此臺灣人利用像是 PChome 和蝦皮購物這類的公司進行網購。在新冠肺炎期間，這幾家和許多其他家網購公司的臺灣訂單都迅速增加。

C **1.**

ⓐ A. **though** [ðo] *conj.* 雖然，儘管
= although [ɔl`ðo]
▸ Though Jason was not handsome, he won the heart of the beautiful woman.
雖然傑森不帥，他仍贏得那美女的芳心。

B. **until** [ʌn`tɪl] *conj.* 直到（= till [tɪl]）
▸ We can't leave until the work is done.
我們要到工作做完才能離開。

C. **whether** [`(h)wɛðɚ] *conj.* 不論（本文用法為引導副詞子句，常與 or 並用）
▸ Whether it rains or shines, Peter goes jogging every morning.
不論晴雨，彼得每天早上都去慢跑。

D. **after** [`æftɚ] *conj.* 在……之後
▸ The campus changed a lot after we graduated.
我們畢業之後校園改變了很多。

ⓑ 空格後有 or，根據語意及用法，C 項應為正選。

D **2.**

ⓐ A. **comment** [ˋkɑmɛnt] *n.* 評語，評論（與介詞 on 並用）

make a comment on...　就……發表評論

▸ The professor made a brief comment on Chloe's painting.
教授對克洛伊的畫進行短評。

B. **instant** [ˋɪnstənt] *n.* 頃刻，片刻 & *a.* 立即的

for an instant　那一瞬間

▸ For an instant, Jerry thought he saw his dead uncle.
那一瞬間，傑瑞以為他看到了他過世的叔叔。

C. **growth** [groθ] *n.* 成長（不可數）

▸ Exercise and healthy food are important to a child's growth.
運動和營養的食物對孩子的成長發育十分重要。

D. **purpose** [ˋpɝpəs] *n.* 目的

for the purpose of...　為了……的目的

▸ We saved money for the purposes of our children's education.
我們為了小孩的教育而存錢。

ⓑ 根據語意及用法，D 項應為正選。

B **3.**

ⓐ A. it is not possible to buy everything that people need in Taiwan
在臺灣不可能買到人們所需的一切

B. Taiwanese people use companies such as PChome and Shopee
臺灣人利用像是 PChome 和蝦皮購物這類的公司

C. there has been a push for Amazon to sell more items in Taiwan
一直有叫亞馬遜在臺灣多販售一些產品的呼聲

D. people in Taiwan ask relatives in other countries to send them goods
臺灣人會請在其他國家的親戚寄貨給他們

ⓑ 根據空格前一句 "Although Amazon can ship some goods to Taiwan, there is no Amazon Taiwan."（雖然亞馬遜可以將某些商品運到臺灣，不過並沒有亞馬遜臺灣區網站。），且 B 項置入空格後較符合上下文語意，故應為正選。

A **4.**

ⓐ 本題測試感官動詞 see（看到）的固定用法：

see + sb/sth + 原形動詞　看到某人／某物做……（強調事實）

▸ Kyle saw the thief steal the woman's purse.
凱爾看到那個小偷偷了那位婦人的皮包。

ⓑ 根據上述，A 項應為正選。

🏷 重要單字片語

1. **hit** [hɪt] *vt.* 侵襲；打擊（三態同形）

2. **unable** [ʌnˋebḷ] *a.* 不能……的
   be unable to V　不能／無法做……

3. **rather** [ˋræðɚ] *adv.* 相反地

4. **goods** [gʊdz] *n.* 商品；貨物（恆用複數，不可數）

5. **millions of...**　　數百萬的……

6. **available** [əˋveləbḷ] *a.* 可利用的；可得到的

7. **push** [pʊʃ] *n.* 敦促（恆用單數）；努力

📖 閱讀理解

This is a story about Tom. Tom was a 15-year-old boy who lived with his parents. His mom and dad did everything for him, including cooking, cleaning, and shopping. Tom never had to lift a finger. One day, though, Tom's mom and dad were both ill. Tom's mom asked him to go to the supermarket to do the food shopping. She told him to get three apples, five carrots, two bottles of juice, and some bananas. She asked him to write a list, but Tom said he was confident he could remember everything. However, when he got to the supermarket, Tom struggled to remember what his mom had said. Was it five apples and three bottles of juice? Or was it five bananas and three carrots? In the end, Tom bought five apples, three carrots, three bottles of juice, and some bananas. When he arrived home with the shopping, Tom's mom just rolled her eyes. Tom realized that he needed a lot more practice helping out around the house!

這是湯姆的故事。湯姆是個跟爸媽住的十五歲男孩。他的爸媽幫他把所有事都做好了，包括做飯、打掃和購物。湯姆從來都不需要幫忙。然而有一天湯姆的爸媽都生病了。媽媽叫他去超市採買食物。她要湯姆買三顆蘋果、五根胡蘿蔔、兩瓶果汁和一些香蕉。她要他寫一張清單，但湯姆說他有把握自己能記住所有東西。不過湯姆到了超市後，很難想起來媽媽的叮嚀。是五顆蘋果和三瓶果汁？還是五根香蕉和三根胡蘿蔔？最後，湯姆買了五顆蘋果、三根胡蘿蔔、三瓶果汁和一些香蕉。湯姆帶著買好的東西回到家時，媽媽直翻白眼。湯姆了解到他需要更多的練習來分攤家裡的工作！

A 1. Which of the following would be the most fitting title for the story?
   A. *A Boy Learns a Lesson*
   B. *A Boy with a Great Memory*
   C. *A Serious Illness in the Family*
   D. *A Family Trip to the Supermarket*

下列何者會是最適合本故事的標題？
A. 學到教訓的小男孩
B. 記性超強的小男孩
C. 家族的嚴重疾病
D. 一家人逛超市

理由

問題類型： 主旨題

本文第一至三句描述一個名叫湯姆的男孩從來不用幫忙家事，第四句至倒數第二句敘述有一天湯姆的父母因生病而需要他幫忙採買東西，他因為過度自信而未正確買到母親要求的東西，文末則說道 "Tom realized that he needed a lot more practice helping out around the house! " （湯姆了解到他需要更多的練習來分攤家裡的工作！），故 A 項應為正選。

C **2.** Why did Tom not write the food items on a list?

A. He couldn't find a pen and paper.

B. He wanted his father to go with him.

C. He was sure he wouldn't forget them.

D. He planned to order them on the internet.

湯姆為什麼不把要買的食物寫在一張清單上？

A. 他找不到紙筆。

B. 他想要他父親陪他去。

C. 他確信自己不會忘記那些東西。

D. 他打算在網路上訂購。

理由

問題類型： 細節題

根 據 本 文 第 八 句 "She asked him to write a list, but Tom said he was confident he could remember everything." （她要他寫一張清單，但湯姆說他有把握自己能記住所有東西。），得知 C 項應為正選。

B **3.** Which of the following shopping lists shows what Tom should have bought?

A.
```
        Shopping List
  · 5 apples
  · 3 carrots
  · 3 bottles of juice
  · bananas
```

B.
```
        Shopping List
  · 3 apples
  · 5 carrots
  · 2 bottles of juice
  · bananas
```

C.
```
        Shopping List
  · 5 apples
  · 2 carrots
  · 3 bottles of juice
  · bananas
```

D.
```
        Shopping List
  · 3 apples
  · 3 carrots
  · 2 bottles of juice
  · bananas
```

下列哪一張購物清單顯示了湯姆原本該要買的東西？

A.
購物清單
・五顆蘋果
・三根胡蘿蔔
・三瓶果汁
・香蕉

B.
購物清單
・三顆蘋果
・五根胡蘿蔔
・兩瓶果汁
・香蕉

C.
購物清單
・五顆蘋果
・兩根胡蘿蔔
・三瓶果汁
・香蕉

D.
購物清單
・三顆蘋果
・三根胡蘿蔔
・兩瓶果汁
・香蕉

理由

問題類型： 細節題

根據本文第七句 "She told him to get three apples, five carrots, two bottles of juice, and some bananas."（她要湯姆買三顆蘋果、五根胡蘿蔔、兩瓶果汁和一些香蕉。），得知 B 項應為正選。

🏷 重要單字片語

1. **lift** [lɪft] *vt.* 抬起，舉起
   lift a finger　幫一點忙，盡舉手之勞

2. **carrot** [ˋkærət] *n.* 胡蘿蔔

3. **confident** [ˋkɑnfədənt] *a.* 有把握的；
   自信的

4. **struggle** [ˋstrʌgl̩] *vi.* 努力；掙扎
   struggle to V　努力做……

5. **roll** [rol] *vt.* 翻（白眼）；（使）滾動
   roll one's eyes　某人翻白眼

6. **help out**　分擔工作；幫忙

7. **fitting** [ˋfɪtɪŋ] *a.* 合適的，恰當的

Unit 9 Leisure Activities 休閒活動

三 段落填空

Free time is very important in our lives. The activities we do outside of school or work can have a big __(1)__ on our health and happiness. These activities might include playing sports, meeting family and friends, or just watching TV. A recent study suggests that young men spend more time on fun activities than young women. The study looked at nearly 900 Spanish people __(2)__ 18 to 24. It found that men have 113 minutes of free time every weekday, __(3)__ women have 101 minutes. __(4)__ , but it adds up to 52 hours every year.

空閒時間在我們的人生中極為重要。我們在上學或工作之餘所從事的活動，對我們的健康與快樂有很大的影響。這些活動可能包括從事體育運動、和親朋好友聚會或僅只是看電視。最近一項研究指出，年輕男性花在休閒活動上的時間高於年輕女性。這項研究的對象是將近九百位年齡為十八到二十四歲的西班牙人。研究發現，男性每個工作天中有一百一十三分鐘的空閒時間，而女性則有一百零一分鐘。這聽起來可能沒有太大的差別，但一整年下來差距高達五十二小時。

__C__ **1.**

ⓐ A. **target** [ˈtɑrgɪt] *n*. 目標
   ▶ The team is confident that they'll hit their sales target next season.
   這個團隊有信心他們下一季能達到銷售目標。

B. **value** [ˈvæljʊ] *n*. 價值；價值觀
   ▶ Renoir's paintings have great artistic value.
   雷諾瓦的畫作具有很高的藝術價值。

C. **effect** [ɪˈfɛkt] *n*. 影響；效果；結果
   have an effect on...   對……有影響
   = have an influence on...
   ▶ Smoking will certainly have a bad effect on your health.
   抽菸對你的健康絕對有不良的影響。

D. **method** [ˈmɛθəd] *n*. 方法
   ▶ Jogging is the simplest and most effective method of exercise.
   慢跑是最簡單也最有效的一種運動方式。

ⓑ 根據上述，C 項應為正選。

A **2.**

ⓐ 原句實為：

The study looked at nearly 900 Spanish people <u>who are aged</u> 18 to 24.

限定修飾的形容詞子句（即關係代名詞之前無逗點）中，若關係代名詞作主詞，該形容詞子句可依下列步驟簡化為分詞片語，步驟如下：

(1) 刪除關係代名詞；

(2) 後面的動詞改為現在分詞（若動詞為 be 動詞，則改為現在分詞 being 後可予省略）。

ⓑ 根據上述，who are aged 可簡化為 aged，故 A 項應為正選。

D **3.**

ⓐ 空格前後兩句分別為 "... men have 113 minutes of free time every weekday"（男性每個工作天中有一百一十三分鐘的空閒時間）及 "women have 101 minutes"（女性則有一百零一分鐘），兩句描述對照的事實，選項中僅 D 項 while（而）可用於連接語意對照的句子。

ⓑ 根據上述，D 項應為正選。

B **4.**

ⓐ A. Children will be included in the next study
下一項研究中將包含孩童

B. This might not sound like much of a difference
這聽起來可能沒有太大的差別

C. Women have to do more jobs around the house
女性得做比較多家事

D. This is because men have many different interests
這是因為男性的興趣廣泛

ⓑ 前句提及研究的結果 "... men have 113 minutes of free time every weekday, while women have 101 minutes."（……男性每個工作天中有一百一十三分鐘的空閒時間，而女性則有一百零一分鐘），而本句後半句敘述 "but it adds up to 52 hours every year"（但一整年下來差距高達五十二小時），得知空格內的敘述應和研究數據有關且與後半句語意對照，B 項置入空格後符合前後文語意，故應為正選。

🏷️ **重要單字片語**

1. **include** [ɪnˈklud] *vt.* 包括

2. **nearly** [ˈnɪrlɪ] *adv.* 幾近；幾乎，差一點

3. **add up to...** 總計為……

📖 **閱讀理解**

There are many things that can affect our choice of free-time activities. One of these, of course, is our own personal interests. Another is how light or dark it is outside. For instance, you may enjoy running, but you do it more during the summer when the evenings are lighter. In around 70 countries in the world, the governments make sure that the evenings are even lighter during the summer. They do this by using daylight saving time. This means that the clocks are moved forward one hour in spring and then put back one hour in the autumn. In the US, it is commonly described as "spring forward, fall back." The result is that countries—mainly in North America and Europe—give their people an extra hour of natural light in the evenings to enjoy their free time. Daylight saving time was first introduced in the UK and US for a reason quite different from today. It was to save energy during the First World War.

影響我們選擇休閒活動的因素很多。其中之一當然是我們個人的興趣。另外一項是戶外天色的明暗。例如你可能喜歡跑步，但你會比較常在夏天從事這項活動，那時傍晚天色較亮。全世界大約有七十個國家的政府想要確保夏天傍晚的天色比正常情況還要亮。他們藉由夏令時間（日光節約時間）來做到這一點。這意味在春天時把時鐘往前撥快一小時，到了秋天再往回撥一小時。在美國，這一般被描述為「往前跳，往後倒」。結果各國 —— 主要是北美和歐洲國家 —— 在傍晚時分給民眾多一小時的晝長來享受閒暇時光。日光節約時間最早在英國和美國實行的原因與今日大不相同。那時是為了在第一次世界大戰中節約能源。

__C__ **1.** Why is running talked about in the article?

　A. It is an example of a very healthy free-time activity.

　B. It is an activity that can only be done during the summer.

　C. It is an example of an activity that can be affected by the light.

　D. It is an activity that is enjoyed in some countries more than others.

本文為何提到跑步？

A. 它是一個極健康休閒活動的例子。

B. 它是一種只有在夏天才能從事的活動。

C. 它是一個會受光線影響的活動的實例。

D. 它是一種在某些國家受歡迎程度勝過其他國家的活動。

理由

問題類型： 推論題

根據本文第四句 "For instance, you may enjoy running, but you do it more during the summer when the evenings are lighter."（例如你可能喜歡跑步，但你會比較常在夏天從事這項活動，那時傍晚天色較亮。），得知 C 項應為正選。

D **2.** What is the writer's personal opinion of daylight saving time?

A. Every country should use it.

B. It should be used all year round.

C. It is a mistake that should be stopped.

D. No personal opinion was given in the article.

> 作者對於夏令時間的個人看法為何？
>
> A. 每個國家都應該採用。
>
> B. 一整年都該採用。
>
> C. 這是一個錯誤，應該停止實施。
>
> D. 文中沒有提到任何個人看法。

理由

問題類型：__細節題__

本文第一至四句提及天色是選擇休閒活動的考量之一，第五至最後一句敘述夏令時間的好處及相關細節，全文未提及作者個人對夏令時間的看法，得知 D 項應為正選。

D **3.** Why was daylight saving time first introduced?

A. To confuse the enemy during a time of war

B. To give people more time to enjoy themselves

C. To make different countries follow the same time

D. To stop people using too much energy during a war

> 最初實行夏令時間的原因是什麼？
>
> A. 在戰時混淆敵人的視聽
>
> B. 給大家更多休閒活動的時間
>
> C. 讓不同國家遵循相同的時間
>
> D. 防止人們在戰爭期間使用過多能源

理由

問題類型：__細節題__

根據本文最後兩句 "Daylight saving time was first introduced in the UK and US for a reason quite different from today. It was to save energy during the First World War."（日光節約時間最早在英國和美國實行的原因與今日大不相同。那時是為了在第一次世界大戰中節約能源。），得知 D 項應為正選。

🏷️ **重要單字片語**

1. **affect** [əˈfɛkt] *vt.* 影響

2. **personal** [ˈpɝsn̩l] *a.* 私人的，個人的

3. **government** [ˈgʌvɚnmənt] *n.* 政府；政體

4. **make sure that + S + V** 確保……，保證……

5. **daylight** [ˈdeˌlaɪt] *n.* 日光；白晝
   daylight saving time 夏令時間，日光節約時間

6. **commonly** [ˈkɑmənlɪ] *adv.* 普遍地

7. **describe** [dɪˈskraɪb] *vt.* 描述，形容
   describe A as B 將 A 描述為 B

8. **introduce** [ˌɪntrəˈdjus] *vt.* 推行（法令）；推出（產品等）；介紹
   introduce A to B 把 A 介紹給 B

9. **confuse** [kənˈfjuz] *vt.* 使困惑；混淆
   confuse A with B 將 A 與 B 混淆

10. **enemy** [ˈɛnəmɪ] *n.* 敵人

Unit 10 Office Life 職場面面觀

段落填空

Starting a new company can be expensive. There are lots of things to spend money on, from workers to tools. Many new small companies are choosing to (1) money by not having a fixed office. In place of this, they use what is called a coworking space. This is a room or a building (2) workers from different companies can share office space. In Taiwan, lots of new businesses are started every day. (3) In Taipei, for instance, coworking spaces can be found in Xinyi, Songshan, and Daan, among other areas. Not only (4) a good way to save money, but they also provide opportunities to meet people in your own and other industries.

創立一家新公司成本相當高。很多事情都需要錢 —— 從員工到用具等等。許多新成立的小公司選擇不要固定的辦公室以節省成本。取而代之的是所謂的共享工作空間，是一個房間或一棟大樓，有不同公司的員工在裡面共享辦公空間。在臺灣，每天都有很多的公司行號成立。因此，這些空間現在變得很普遍。例如在臺北，信義區、松山區和大安區等都有共享工作空間。它們不但是省錢的好方法，還提供認識你本業和其他行業的人的機會。

D 1.

ⓐ A. **provide** [prəˈvaɪd] vt. 提供

　　provide sb with sth　　提供某物給某人

　= provide sth for sb

　▸ Jeff provided the poor stranger with food and clothing.
　　傑夫提供食物和衣服給那個可憐的陌生人。

　B. **cash** [kæʃ] vt. 把……兌現 & n. 現金

　　cash a check　　兌現支票

　▸ Can I cash these traveler's checks at this hotel?
　　我能在這間飯店兌換旅行支票嗎？

　C. **deliver** [dɪˈlɪvɚ] vt. 運送，投遞

　▸ That pizza shop delivers pizzas in less than 30 minutes.
　　那間披薩店會在三十分鐘內將披薩送達。

　D. **save** [sev] vt. 節省；拯救

　▸ We travel by plane to save time.
　　我們搭飛機旅行以節省時間。

ⓑ 根據語意，得知 D 項應為正選。

C **2.**

ⓐ 空格前有完整句子 This is a room or a building（這是一個房間或一棟大樓），空格後有另一完整句子 workers from different companies can share office space（不同公司的員工可以共享辦公空間），得知空格應置指涉「地方」的關係副詞 where（= in which），引導形容詞子句修飾先行詞 a room or a building。

ⓑ A 項 that 為指涉「人事物」的關係代名詞；D 項 which 為指涉「事物」的關係代名詞；B 項 what 為複合關係代名詞，等於 the thing(s) which，表「所……的東西」，使用時其前不可有先行詞；故上述三項皆不可選。

ⓒ 根據上述，C 項應為正選。

A **3.**

ⓐ A. Therefore, these spaces are becoming very common.
因此，這些空間現在變得很普遍。

B. However, there are none of these spaces in Taiwan.
然而，臺灣沒有這種空間。

C. Still, goods are exported to many different countries.
儘管如此，商品仍出口到許多不同的國家。

D. As a result, the roads are being improved in the cities.
結果，城市的街道狀況正在進行改善。

ⓑ 根據空格前一句 "In Taiwan, lots of new businesses are started every day."（在臺灣，每天都有很多新的公司行號成立。）及空格後一句 "In Taipei, for instance, coworking spaces can be found in Xinyi, Songshan, and Daan, among other areas."（例如在臺北，信義區、松山區和大安區等都有共享工作空間。），可推知空格應與許多新成立的公司以及共享工作空間有關，A 項置入空格後符合上下文語意，故應為正選。

B **4.**

ⓐ 本題測試 not only... but also... 的固定用法：
not only... but also... 為對等連接詞片語，可連接對等的單字、片語或子句。若連接對等的子句時，由於 not only 視為否定副詞，置句首時所引導的子句要倒裝；而 but also 僅為連接詞，故其後的子句不須倒裝，但 also 可省略，或移至主詞後。亦可將 also 省略後在句尾處加 as well。

▸ Not only was Andrew my classmate, but he was (also) a good friend of mine.
= Not only was Andrew my classmate, but he was a good friend of mine as well.
安德魯不僅是我同學，也是我的好朋友。

ⓑ 根據上述，本句前、後半句的主詞應相同，均為 they，另因空格後為名詞詞組 a good way，得知前半句的主詞 they 之後須接 be 動詞，並採倒裝句構，故 B 項應為正選。

重要單字片語

1. **tool** [tul] *n.* 工具；用具
2. **fixed** [fɪkst] *a.* 固定的
3. **coworking** [ˌkoˋwɝkɪŋ] *n.* 共同工作（空間），共享空間
   co- [ko] *prefix* 和……一起，共同
4. **opportunity** [ˌɑpɚˋtjunətɪ] *n.* 機會
5. **industry** [ˋɪndəstrɪ] *n.* 產業，行業；工業
6. **export** [ɪksˋport] *vt.* 出口，外銷
7. **As a result, S + V** 結果，……
8. **improve** [ɪmˋpruv] *vt. & vi.* 改善

閱讀理解

Julie has always wanted to be a journalist. Ever since she was a little girl, she has dreamed of interviewing famous people and writing reports about important events. She studied to be a journalist for four years in college. While she was there, she wrote articles for the student paper. It took Julie nearly a year to find a job after graduation, but she finally got a position as a reporter at a local newspaper. On her first day, she was introduced to the chief reporter, an old man with glasses. He asked Julie to interview a singer who was visiting their town. Although not a fan of popular music, Julie was sure she knew what the young singer looked like. When she arrived at the meeting place, Julie started questioning the long-haired guy with a beard who was standing to her right. It was only after the fifth question that she realized the singer was the short-haired man with no beard who was standing on her left! Luckily, both the singer and the chief reporter saw the funny side and didn't blame her!

茱莉一直想當新聞記者。她從小就夢想能採訪名人，撰寫重要事件的報導。她在大學花了四年時間學習當記者。在校期間她幫學生報紙寫報導。畢業後，茱莉花了將近一年時間找工作，但終於在一家地方報社得到記者的職位。上班第一天，她被引介給採訪主任，一位戴眼鏡的老先生。他要茱莉採訪一位正在他們鎮上的歌手。茱莉雖然不是流行樂迷，但她確信自己知道這位年輕歌手的外貌。到達會面地點後，茱莉便開始對著站在她右邊那名留鬍子的長髮男子問問題。直到問完第五個問題，她才發現要採訪的歌手是站在她左邊沒鬍子的短髮男！幸好歌手和採訪主任都只覺得好笑而沒有責備她！

<u>A</u> **1.** Which of the following facts about Julie is NOT true?

A. She found a good job as soon as she completed her studies.

B. She was a writer at a newspaper when she was in college.

C. She liked the idea of being a journalist when she was a child.

D. She wouldn't describe herself as being interested in popular music.

關於茱莉，下列哪一項事實不正確？
A. 她一完成學業就找到一份好工作。
B. 她在大學時就當了報紙的撰稿人。
C. 她小時候就喜歡當新聞記者這個想法。
D. 她不會說自己對流行音樂感興趣。

理由

問題類型：　細節題

根 據 本 文 第 五 句 "It took Julie nearly a year to find a job after graduation, but she finally got a position as a reporter at a local newspaper."（畢業後，茱莉花了將近一年時間找工作，但終於在一家地方報社得到記者的職位。），得知 A 項敘述不正確，故應為正選。

<u>B</u> **2.** Which of the pictures shows the singer that Julie should have interviewed?
下列哪一張圖顯示茱莉應該要採訪的歌手？

A.    B.    C.    D.

理由

問題類型：　細節題（圖片題）

根據本文第八句 "Although not a fan of popular music, Julie was sure she knew what the young singer looked like."（茱莉雖然不是流行樂迷，但她確信自己知道這位年輕歌手的外貌。）及倒數第二句 "It was only after the fifth question that she realized the singer was the short-haired man with no beard who was standing on her left!"（直到問完第五個問題，她才發現要採訪的歌手是站在她左邊沒鬍子的短髮男！），得知 B 項應為正選。

CH
1

C **3.** What lesson might Julie have learned from her first day at the newspaper?

    A. She should listen to more rock music.

    B. She should get her hair cut more often.

    C. She should prepare more before an interview.

    D. She should go back to university to take another degree.

茉莉可能從報社上班的第一天學到什麼教訓？

A. 她應該多聽搖滾樂。

B. 她應該更常剪頭髮。

C. 她應該在採訪前做更多準備。

D. 她應該回到大學再拿一個學位。

理由

問題類型： 推論題

本文第六至八句講述茉蒂第一天上班就被交付採訪一位年輕流行樂歌手的工作，她不熟悉流行樂界卻又過度自信而未事先確認該名歌手的長相，接著第九至十句提及茉蒂到了現場後便立即採訪身邊的歌手，後來才發現認錯人了。由此可知茉蒂理應做好事前準備工作，故 **C** 項應為正選。

重要單字片語

1. **journalist** [ˋdʒɝnəlɪst] *n.* 新聞記者

2. **dream of + N/V-ing** 　　夢想／渴望……

3. **interview** [ˋɪntɚˏvju] *vt. & n.* 採訪；面試

4. **position** [pəˋzɪʃən] *n.* 職位，職務；位置

5. **chief** [tʃif] *a.* 首席的 & *n.* 首長，領導人

6. **as soon as...** 一……（就……）

7. **complete** [kəmˋplit] *vt.* 完成

8. **prepare** [prɪˋpɛr] *vi.* 準備 & *vt.* 把……準備好

9. **degree** [dɪˋgri] *n.* 學位；度數

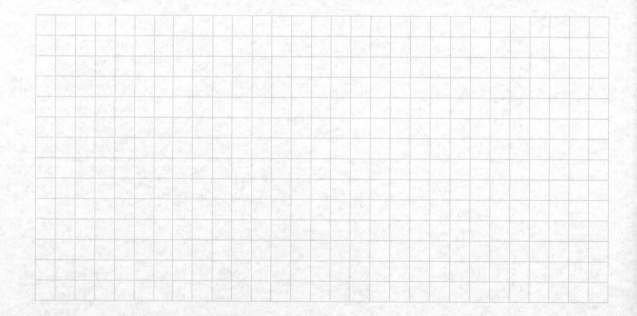

Chapter 1 單篇閱讀 詳解

Part B 生活類

A

Amy & Sam's Vacation Plan

Day	Time of Day	Activity
Monday	Morning	Arrive at the hotel
	Afternoon	Go swimming at the beach
	Evening	Meal at a steak restaurant
Tuesday	Morning	A trip to see mountain lions
	Afternoon	Go walking in the countryside
	Evening	Go dancing at a local bar
Wednesday	Morning	Rest in the hotel
	Afternoon	Go swimming in the hotel pool
	Evening	Meal in the hotel restaurant
Thursday	Morning	A trip to see a local church
	Afternoon	Gift shopping in local shops
	Evening	Meal at an expensive restaurant

艾咪和山姆的度假計畫

星期	時段	活動
星期一	早上	到達飯店
	下午	海邊游泳
	晚上	牛排館用餐
星期二	早上	看山獅
	下午	到鄉間走走
	晚上	在地酒吧跳舞
星期三	早上	飯店休息
	下午	飯店游泳池游泳
	晚上	飯店餐廳用餐
星期四	早上	參觀在地教堂
	下午	在地商店買禮品
	晚上	高檔餐廳用餐

CH
1

__C__ **1.** On which day will Amy and Sam spend the most time at their hotel?
A. Monday
B. Tuesday
C. Wednesday
D. Thursday

艾咪和山姆哪一天大部分的時間會待在飯店裡？
A. 星期一
B. 星期二
C. 星期三
D. 星期四

理由

問題類型：細節題

根據計畫表，星期三早上的行程為 Rest in the hotel（飯店休息），下午的行程為 Go swimming in the hotel pool（飯店游泳池游泳），晚上的行程為 Meal in the hotel restaurant（飯店餐廳用餐），得知 C 項應為正選。

__B__ **2.** Which of the following is NOT true about Amy and Sam's vacation?
A. They will spend some time by the coast.
B. They will play a sport with local people.
C. They will visit an important local building.
D. They will go to see some animals in the hills.

關於艾咪和山姆的假期，下列哪一項敘述不正確？
A. 他們會在海邊待一段時間。
B. 他們會和當地人進行體育活動。
C. 他們會參觀當地一棟重要建築。
D. 他們會去山裡看一些動物。

理由

問題類型：細節題

計畫表第三、第十一及第五列分別提到 A、C、D 項，整個表未提及將和當地人一起運動，故 B 項應為正選。

__C__ **3.** When will Amy and Sam most likely buy presents for their friends?
A. On Tuesday evening
B. On Monday morning
C. On Thursday afternoon
D. On Wednesday afternoon

艾咪和山姆最有可能在什麼時間賞禮物給朋友？
A. 星期二晚上
B. 星期一早上
C. 星期四下午
D. 星期三下午

理由

問題類型：細節題

根據計畫表，星期四下午的行程為 Gift shopping in local shops（在地商店買禮品），得知 C 項應為正選。

🏷 重要單字片語

1.	**arrive at...**	到達（車站、建築物等）	
	arrive in...	到達（城市、國家等）	
2.	**local** [ˋlokḷ] *a.* 當地的，本地的		

3. **bar** [bɑr] *n.* 酒吧；吧臺；棒；條

4. **coast** [kost] *n.* 海岸

5. **hill** [hɪl] *n.* 山丘，小山

B

Train Schedule

Place	Train 1A	Train 2B	Train 3C	Train 4D
Great Town	07:47	08:53	09:25	10:01
Church Hill	07:57	09:03	09:35	10:11
Hazel River	08:00	09:06	09:38	10:14
Springfield	08:15	09:21	09:53	10:29
Capitol City	08:35	09:41	10:13	10:49

➢ *Changes to train times:*

- *The second train of the day is canceled because of a lack of customers.*

- *The third train of the day no longer stops at Church Hill.*

- *All trains will arrive at Capitol City ten minutes late because of track repair work.*

火車時刻表

地點	車次 1A	車次 2B	車次 3C	車次 4D
大鎮	07:47	08:53	09:25	10:01
教堂山	07:57	09:03	09:35	10:11
榛樹河	08:00	09:06	09:38	10:14
春田	08:15	09:21	09:53	10:29
首府	08:35	09:41	10:13	10:49

➢ *火車時刻變動：*

- 當天第二車次因旅客人數過少取消。

- 當天第三車次將不停靠教堂山站。

- 因鐵軌維修作業，停靠首府站的所有車次均將晚十分鐘到站。

C **1.** Which train will go straight from Great Town to Hazel River?

    A. Train 1A

    B. Train 2B

    C. Train 3C

    D. Train 4D

哪一車次會從大鎮直達榛樹河？

    A. 車次 1A

    B. 車次 2B

    C. 車次 3C

    D. 車次 4D

理由

問題類型： 細節題

根據時刻表下方的説明事項第二點，"The third train of the day no longer stops at Church Hill."（當天第三車次將不停靠教堂山站。），得知車次 3C 從大鎮站出發後會直達榛樹河站，故 C 項應為正選。

D **2.** Why will Train 4D arrive at Capitol City at 10:59?

    A. There are too many people wanting to travel.

    B. There are more stops being added after Springfield.

    C. There are not enough workers to sell tickets at the station.

    D. There are delays because work is being done on the track.

車次 4D 為什麼會在十點五十九分才到達首府？

    A. 有太多人想搭乘。

    B. 過春田站後有更多停靠站加入。

    C. 車站裡沒有足夠的售票員工。

    D. 因為進行鐵軌工程而延誤。

理由

問題類型： 細節題

根據時刻表下方的第三點説明，"All trains will arrive at Capitol City ten minutes late because of track repair work."（因鐵軌維修作業，停靠首府站的所有車次均將晚十分鐘到站。），得知 D 項應為正選。

A **3.** James boards the train at Great Town. His office is a fifteen-minute walk from Springfield. Which train does James have to take if he wants to get to the office before 10 o'clock?

    A. 07:47

    B. 08:53

    C. 09:25

    D. He can't catch any train.

詹姆士在大鎮站上車。他的辦公室離春田站走路要十五分鐘。如果詹姆士要在十點前到公司，該搭幾點的火車？

    A. 七點四十七分

    B. 八點五十三分

    C. 九點二十五分

    D. 沒有適合的班次可搭乘。

理由

問題類型： 情境題

根據題幹敘述，詹姆士須預留十五分鐘從車站步行至公司，也就是須在九點四十五分前到達公司附近的春田站，根據時刻表，從大鎮站出發、九點四十五分前到達春田站的車次有 1A 及 2B，惟根據時刻表下方的說明事項第一點 "The second train of the day is canceled because of a lack of customers."（當天第二車次因旅客人數過少取消。），得知車次 2B 已取消，詹姆士僅能搭乘車次 1A，故 A 項應為正選。

📎 重要單字片語

1. **cancel** [ˈkænsḷ] *vt.* 取消（= call off）
2. **lack** [læk] *n. & vt.* 缺乏
   a lack of sth　　缺乏某物
3. **no longer**　　不再
4. **because of + N/V-ing**　　因為……
5. **track** [træk] *n.*（鐵路的）軌道；小徑 & *vt.* 追蹤
6. **repair** [rɪˈpɛr] *n. & vt.* 修繕；修理
7. **delay** [dɪˈle] *n. & vt.* 延誤；延期

A

Jenna < Hi, Eric! How was your first day at the new school?

It was OK, thanks. The teachers and the classmates were all welcoming, but I miss my old friends. > **Eric**

Jenna < We miss you, too! School's not the same without you. What am I going to do in science class without you there helping me?

I know it's not your best subject, haha! I can still help you, though. Ask me anything here if you need me. > **Eric**

Jenna < Thanks, Eric. You're the best!

珍娜 < 嗨，艾瑞克！你在新學校的第一天還好嗎？

還不錯，謝謝。這裡的老師和同學人都很熱情友善，可我還是很想念老朋友。 > 艾瑞克

珍娜 < 我們也想你啊！沒了你，上課的感覺都不一樣了。自然課沒有你在那裡幫我，都不知道該怎麼辦。

我知道自然科不是你最拿手的科目，哈哈！不過我還是可以幫妳呀。需要我的時候就在這裡問我嘛。 > 艾瑞克

珍娜 < 艾瑞克，謝啦。你人最好了！

D **1.** What do we learn about Jenna and Eric?

A. They are classmates now.

B. They have never met before.

C. They used to date and were a couple.

D. They no longer attend the same school.

關於珍娜和艾瑞克，我們得知什麼？

A. 他們現在是同學。

B. 他們從未見過面。

C. 他們以前約會過，曾是情侶。

D. 他們不再就讀同一間學校。

理由

問題類型：推論題

根據本對話開頭珍娜的問候 "Hi, Eric! How was your first day at the new school?（嗨，艾瑞克！你在新學校的第一天還好嗎？）及第三段珍娜的回應 "We miss you, too! School's not the same without you."（我們也想你啊！沒了你，上課的感覺都不一樣了。），可推知艾瑞克已從原本跟珍娜一起就讀的學校轉學了，故 D 項應為正選。

A 2. What is Eric's opinion of his new school?

    A. He thinks everyone is friendly.

    B. He thinks the work is too hard.

    C. He thinks the people aren't nice.

    D. He thinks it has too many students.

艾瑞克對新學校的看法如何？

A. 他覺得大家都很友善。

B. 他覺得課業太難。

C. 他覺得那裡的人不親切。

D. 他覺得學生太多。

理由

問題類型： 細節題

根據本對話第二段艾瑞克的回覆 "It was OK, thanks. The teachers and the classmates were all welcoming, but I miss my old friends."（還不錯，謝謝。這裡的老師和同學人都很熱情友善，可我還是很想念老朋友。），得知 A 項應為正選。

B 3. Why is Jenna pleased with Eric?

    A. Because he is going to visit her

    B. Because he promises to help her

    C. Because he tells her she is clever

    D. Because he answered a hard question

珍娜為什麼對艾瑞克很滿意？

A. 因為他要去看她

B. 因為他允諾幫助她

C. 因為他對她說她很聰明

D. 因為他回答了一個很難的問題

理由

問題類型： 細節題

根據本對話第三段第三句珍娜的詢問 "What am I going to do in science class without you there helping me?"（自然課沒有你在那裡幫我，都不知道該怎麼辦。）及下一段艾瑞克回覆的第二、三句 "I can still help you, though. Ask me anything here if you need me."（不過我還是可以幫妳呀。需要我的時候就在這裡問我嘛。），得知 B 項應為正選。

🏷 **重要單字片語**

1. **welcoming** [ˋwɛlkəmɪŋ] *a.* 友好的，熱情的

2. **science** [ˋsaɪəns] *n.* 自然科學；科學

3. **used to V** 過去曾經 / 常常做……

4. **date** [det] *vi.* 約會，談戀愛 & *vt.* 與（某人）約會 & *n.* 約會

5. **couple** [ˋkʌpḷ] *n.* 情侶；夫妻

6. **be pleased with...** 對……感到滿意

7. **promise** [ˋprɑmɪs] *vt.* 承諾，答應
   promise to V 承諾做……

8. **clever** [ˋklɛvɚ] *a.* 聰明的；機伶的

B

Wally Welcome to our music group!

Thank you! **Olivia**

Wally If you have any questions, please let me know.

Actually, I was wondering if you guys ever meet up in person to listen to music together. **Olivia**

Wally Not really, no. We just use this room to talk about our favorite artists and introduce new music to others.

OK, thanks. What are your favorite types of music, Wally? **Olivia**

Wally I love hard rock and heavy metal. What about you?

I like all kinds of music! **Olivia**

瓦力 歡迎加入我們的音樂群組！

謝謝！ 奧莉薇亞

瓦力 有任何問題可以問我。

說真的，我想知道你們會不會見面然後一起聽音樂。 奧莉薇亞

瓦力 不會。我們只在這個聊天室討論自己最喜歡的音樂人，順便介紹新的音樂給其他人。

了解，謝謝。瓦力，你最喜歡哪些類型的音樂？ 奧莉薇亞

瓦力 我喜歡重搖滾和重金屬。妳呢？

我各種音樂都喜歡！ 奧莉薇亞

C **1.** Who most likely is Wally?
  A. The brother of Olivia
  B. A famous music artist
  C. The leader of the group
  D. A new member of the group

瓦力最有可能是誰？
  A. 奧莉薇亞的哥哥
  B. 一位知名音樂人
  C. 該群組的版主
  D. 該群組的新成員

理由

問題類型：推論題

根據本對話，瓦力一開始便主動歡迎奧莉薇亞的加入並歡迎她發問，而且熟知該群組的一切，可推知 C 項應為正選。

A **2. What do we find out about the group?**
    A. It does not meet in person.
    B. It doesn't accept new members.
    C. It has been recently formed.
    D. It focuses on one type of music.

關於這個群組，我們可以得知什麼？
A. 其成員不會見面。
B. 它不接受新成員。
C. 它最近才成立。
D. 它專門聽某一類型的音樂。

理由

問題類型：細節題

根據本對話第四段奧莉維亞的提問 "Actually, I was wondering if you guys ever meet up in person to listen to music together."（說真的，我想知道你們會不會見面然後一起聽音樂。）及瓦力的回答 "Not really, no. We just use this room to talk about our favorite artists and introduce new music to others."（不會。我們只在這個聊天室討論自己最喜歡的音樂人，順便介紹新的音樂給其他人。），得知 A 項應為正選。

B **3. What is true about Wally's tastes in music?**
    A. He enjoys easy-listening music.
    B. He likes certain types of music.
    C. He enjoys his own band's music.
    D. He likes different kinds of music.

關於瓦力的音樂品味，下列何者正確？
A. 他喜歡輕音樂。
B. 他喜歡某些類型的音樂。
C. 他喜歡自己樂團的音樂。
D. 他喜歡不同種類的音樂。

理由

問題類型：細節題

根據本對話倒數第二段瓦力的回答 "I love hard rock and heavy metal."（我喜歡重搖滾和重金屬。），得知他喜歡一些節奏較強烈的音樂，故 B 項應為正選。

🏷️ **重要單字片語**

1. **actually** [ˋæktʃuəlɪ] *adv.* 實際上，其實
2. **meet up** 碰面
3. **in person** 親自；本人
4. **artist** [ˋɑrtɪst] *n.* 藝人；藝術家
5. **hard rock** 重搖滾

6. **heavy metal** 重金屬搖滾樂
7. **accept** [əkˋsɛpt] *vt.* 接受，接納
8. **focus on...** 著重於／聚焦在……
9. **easy-listening** [ˋizɪˋlɪsənɪŋ] *a.* 輕鬆悅耳的
    easy listening 輕音樂

A

Sandtown Movie Theater Presents

TWO MATCHES MADE TO LAST

Screen: Number Two
Seat: Number 7A

Admit One

Adult Price: $10 / Child Price: $7 / Student Price: $6 / Senior Price: $5

Please note that smoking is not allowed in the movie theater.
Please turn your phone on silent before the start of the movie.
Please take away your trash at the end of the movie.
You are not allowed to record any part of the movie—
anyone caught doing so will be told to leave the movie theater.

沙城電影院隆重獻映

《天長地久一對寶》

放映廳：二廳
座位：7A

單人票價

成人票：十美元 / 孩童票：七美元 / 學生票：六美元 / 敬老票：五美元

請注意：戲院內禁止吸菸。
電影開演前請將手機調至靜音。
電影結束後請將垃圾帶走。
禁止攝錄任何電影片段 ——
違者將被要求離場。

A **1.** What do we learn about Sandtown Movie Theater?

　A. It has more than one screen.

　B. It is the only theater in town.

　C. It only shows one movie at a time.

　D. It does not allow eating or drinking.

關於沙城電影院，我們得知哪一項？

A. 院內的放映廳不只一間。

B. 是城裡唯一一間戲院。

C. 一次只放映一部電影。

D. 院內禁止飲食。

理由

問題類型：推論題

根據票券第三行 "**Screen:** Number Two"（**放映廳**：二廳），得知該電影院的放映廳不只一間，故 A 項應為正選。

B **2.** Kerry goes to the local university. How much does she have to pay to see a movie?

　A. $5

　B. $6

　C. $7

　D. $10

凱莉在當地上大學。她看電影要付多少錢？

A. 五美元

B. 六美元

C. 七美元

D. 十美元

理由

問題類型：情境題

根據票券第六行中的 "Student Price: $6"（學生票：六美元），得知 B 項應為正選。

D **3.** Based on the ticket, why might you be told to leave the movie theater?

　A. You have created too much garbage.

　B. You have smoked outside the theater.

　C. You have been caught talking to your friend.

　D. You have been discovered recording the movie.

根據這張票券，你可能會因為什麼原因被要求離開戲院？

A. 你製造了太多垃圾。

B. 你在戲院外吸菸。

C. 你被發現和朋友說話。

D. 你被發現偷錄電影。

理由

問題類型：細節題

根據票券最後一句 "You are not allowed to record any part of the movie—anyone caught doing so will be told to leave the movie theater."（禁止攝錄任何電影片段 —— 違者將被要求離場。），得知 D 項應為正選。

🏷️ 重要單字片語

1. **screen** [skrin] *n.* 螢幕；銀幕（本文中指電影的放映廳）

2. **admit** [əd`mɪt] *vt.* 准許入場／入學；容許，許可；承認

3. **senior** [`sinjə] *n.* 年長者；大四大學生 & *a.* 年長的；地位較高的

4. **allow** [ə`laʊ] *vt.* 允許，讓
   allow sb to V　允許某人做……

5. **silent** [`saɪlənt] *n.* 靜音（模式）& *a.* 無聲的，安靜的；沉默的

   turn / put / set sb's phone on silent
   將某人的手機調至靜音

6. **at a time**　一次

7. **university** [ˌjunə`vɝsətɪ] *n.* 大學

8. **create** [krɪ`et] *vt.* 創造；創作

9. **garbage** [`ɡɑrbɪdʒ] *n.* 垃圾（不可數）（美式用法）

10. **discover** [dɪs`kʌvə] *vt.* 發現

CH 1

B

The Super American Football Center

LEA TOWN LIONS vs. CLINT CITY CATS

Friday, November 5th, 2021

7:30 p.m.

Section B / Line 10 / Seat 18

Admit One

Standard Price: $50 / Member Price: $30

Notes:
The Super American Football Center advises arriving half an hour before game time.
Members are asked to show their member card along with their ticket in order to be charged the lower price.
No outside food or drinks are allowed in the center.

超級美式足球中心

立亞城雄獅隊 對抗 克林特市猛貓隊

2021 年十一月五日星期五

晚上七點三十分

B 區 / 第十排 / 十八號座位

單人票價

一般票價：五十美元 / 會員票價：三十美元

注意：

超級美式足球中心建議您在開賽半小時前到場。

會員須出示會員卡和入場券，方能享有優惠票價。

場內禁帶外食。

C **1.** What is NOT true about the football game on the ticket?

  A. People will sit in different sections.

  B. It takes place on a weekday evening.

  C. People are advised to arrive at 7:30 p.m.

  D. The teams have names based on animals.

票券上關於足球比賽的敘述哪一項不正確？

  A. 人們會坐在不同的區塊。

  B. 比賽在週間的晚上舉行。

  C. 建議觀眾在晚上七點半到場。

  D. 球隊是以動物來命名。

理由

問題類型： 細節題

根據票券第四行的比賽時間 7:30 p.m.（晚上七點三十分）及注意事項第一行 "The Super American Football Center advises arriving half an hour before game time."（超級美式足球中心建議您在開賽半小時前到場。），得知中心建議觀眾七點到達現場，故 C 項敘述錯誤，應為正選。

D **2.** How can someone pay thirty dollars to see the game?

  A. Win a prize

  B. Arrive early

  C. Buy two tickets

  D. Become a member

要如何以三十美元的票價進場看球？

  A. 贏得獎項

  B. 提早到場

  C. 買兩張票

  D. 成為會員

理由

問題類型： 細節題

根據票券第七行中的票價 Member Price: $30（會員票價：三十美元），得知 D 項應為正選。

C **3.** Based on the ticket, what can people probably do if they want to eat food at the game?

    A. Order it from a restaurant

    B. Bring it from their own home

    C. Get it from inside the sports center

    D. Buy it from a food truck outside

根據這張票券，若想在比賽現場吃東西，可能會怎麼做？

A. 向餐廳訂餐

B. 從自家帶來

C. 在運動中心裡購買

D. 向場外的餐車購買

CH 1

理由

問題類型： 推論題

根據票券最後一行 "No outside food or drinks are allowed in the center."（場內禁帶外食。），得知 C 項應為正選。

🏷️ 重要單字片語

1. **section** [ˈsɛkʃən] *n.* 區域；部分（= part）；部門

2. **standard** [ˈstændɚd] *a.* 標準的 & *n.* 標準，水準，模範

3. **advise** [ədˈvaɪz] *vt.* 勸告，忠告；通知
   advise + N/V-ing　建議……
   advise sb (not) to V　勸某人（不要）做……

4. **along with...**　和……一起

5. **charge** [tʃɑrdʒ] *vt. & vi.* 索（費）；充電；指控 & *n.* 索費；指控；負責
   charge sb + 價錢（+ for sth）
   （為某事物）向某人索價若干錢

6. **take place**　（事件）舉行；發生

Ⓐ

From:	office.manager@karens.kitchens.com
To:	office.staff@karens.kitchens.com
Subject:	Please Clean Up

Hi All,

Firstly, the cleaner has asked me to remind you that it is not her job to wash your dirty dishes. Please do not leave half-empty coffee cups or half-eaten sandwiches on your desks. These might encourage insects. The cleaner is here to empty the trash and make sure the shared areas are clean. Secondly, the parking lot will be closing early tonight at 6 p.m. Please make sure that you leave before this time.

Thank you.

Leah Vincent

寄件者：	office.manager@karens.kitchens.com
收件者：	office.staff@karens.kitchens.com
主　旨：	請收拾乾淨

大家好：

第一件事，清潔工請我提醒各位，她沒有義務清洗你們的髒碗盤。請不要把喝了一半的咖啡杯或吃了一半的三明治留在辦公桌上。這些東西可能會招來蟲子。清潔工是來清空垃圾桶並確保公共區域清潔的。第二件事，停車場今天會提早在傍晚六點關閉。請務必在這個時間之前離開。

謝謝。

莉亞・文森

<u>C</u> **1.** What is the main topic of the email?

A. The hiring of a new cleaner

B. A new coffee shop in the area

C. A message to keep the office clean

D. The problems in the office parking lot

本電子郵件的主題是什麼？

A. 聘僱一位新清潔工

B. 附近的一家新咖啡廳

C. 通知維持辦公室清潔的訊息

D. 辦公室停車場內的問題

CH 1

理由

問題類型： 主旨題

根據本電子郵件開頭的主旨 **Please Clean Up**（請收拾乾淨）及內文第二、三句 "**Please do not leave half-empty coffee cups or half-eaten sandwiches on your desks. These might encourage insects.**"（請不要把喝了一半的咖啡杯或吃了一半的三明治留在辦公桌上。這些東西可能會招來蟲子。），得知 **C** 項應為正選。

<u>B</u> **2.** What is one of the cleaner's jobs?

A. Washing dirty dishes

B. Taking the trash away

C. Cleaning the parking lot

D. Cleaning everyone's desks

該名清潔工的工作之一是什麼？

A. 洗髒碗盤

B. 收垃圾

C. 清理停車場

D. 收拾大家的辦公桌

理由

問題類型： 細節題

根據本電子郵件內文第四句 "**The cleaner is here to empty the trash and make sure the shared areas are clean.**"（清潔工是來清空垃圾桶並確保公共區域清潔的。），得知 **B** 項應為正選。

<u>C</u> **3.** Why are insects discussed in the email?

A. The company sells them as food.

B. There are many in the parking lot.

C. They might enter the office to eat the food.

D. The office used to have a problem with them.

本電子郵件為什麼提到蟲子？

A. 這家公司把牠們當食物販售。

B. 停車場裡有許多蟲子。

C. 牠們可能會跑進辦公室吃裡面的食物。

D. 這間辦公室裡曾經有蟲子方面的問題。

理由

問題類型： 細節題

根據本電子郵件內文第二、三句 "**Please do not leave half-empty coffee cups or half-eaten sandwiches on your desks. These might encourage insects.**"（請不要把喝了一半的咖啡杯或吃了一半的三明治留在辦公桌上。這些東西可能會招來蟲子。），得知 **C** 項應為正選。

🏷 重要單字片語

1. **encourage** [ɪnˈkɜɪdʒ] *vt.* 助長;鼓勵
2. **insect** [ˈɪnsɛkt] *n.* 昆蟲;蟲
3. **a parking lot**　停車場
4. **hiring** [ˈhaɪrɪŋ] *n.* 僱用

B

From:	p.simpson@coldmail.com
To:	g.flanders@zmail.com
Subject:	Hey!

George!

Long time no see, buddy! I don't think I've seen you since Barry's wedding ten years ago. I was looking through the photos the other day, and I realized we hadn't spoken for a while. So, I decided to email you to see how you're doing. Are you still living in California? How are Maggie and the kids? I got a new job as a house painter! I got tired of working in an office and wanted a change. Look forward to hearing from you.

Pete

寄件者：	p.simpson@coldmail.com
收件者：	g.flanders@zmail.com
主　旨：	嘿！

喬治！

好兄弟,好久不見!我好像從十年前貝瑞的婚禮之後就沒再見過你了。前幾天我在翻看老照片,才發覺我們已經很久沒聊聊了,所以我決定發個電郵給你問候一下。你還住在加州嗎?瑪姬和孩子們都好嗎?我找了個新工作,是當房屋油漆工!我厭倦了在辦公室上班,所以想改變一下。期待你的回信。

彼特

CH
1

C **1.** What caused Pete to email George?
    A. He wanted to offer him a job.
    B. He needed to ask him a favor.
    C. He saw him in some old photos.
    D. He wanted to invite him to a wedding.

什麼事情促使彼特發電子郵件給喬治？
A. 他想給他工作。
B. 他需要請他幫個忙。
C. 他在某些舊相片裡看到他。
D. 他想邀請他參加婚禮。

理由

問題類型： 細節題

根據本電子郵件內文第三、四句 "I was looking through the photos the other day, and I realized we hadn't spoken for a while. So, I decided to email you to see how you're doing."（前幾天我在翻看老照片，才發覺我們已經很久沒聊聊了，所以我決定發個電郵給你問候一下。），得知 C 項應為正選。

A **2.** What does Pete NOT ask George about?
    A. His work
    B. How he is
    C. His family
    D. Where he lives

彼特沒有問喬治什麼事情？
A. 他的工作
B. 他過得如何
C. 他的家人
D. 他住哪裡

理由

問題類型： 細節題

根據本電郵內文第四至六句 "So, I decided to email you to see how you're doing. Are you still living in California? How are Maggie and the kids?"（所以我決定發個電郵給你問候一下。你還住在加州嗎？瑪姬和孩子們都好嗎？），得知彼特並未詢問喬治工作方面的事情，故 A 項應為正選。

C **3.** What do we learn about Pete?
    A. He is going to California.
    B. He is married with children.
    C. He has recently changed jobs.
    D. He needs to get his house painted.

關於彼特，我們可以得知什麼？
A. 他要去加州。
B. 他已婚有小孩。
C. 他最近換工作了。
D. 他的房子要粉刷。

理由

問題類型： 細節題

根 據 本 電 郵 內 文 倒 數 第 三 至 二 句 "I got a new job as a house painter! I got tired of working in an office and wanted a change."（我找了個新工作，是當房屋油漆工！我厭倦了在辦公室上班，所以想改變一下。），得知 C 項應為正選。

🏷️ 重要單字片語

1. **Long time no see.** 好久不見。(此慣用語原為早期的中式英語，英美人士現已普遍使用)

2. **buddy** [ˈbʌdɪ] *n.* 夥伴；老兄(對熟朋友的稱呼，複數形為 buddies)

3. **the other day** 日昨，前幾天(用於過去的狀況)

4. **for a while** 有一陣子／一會兒

5. **get / be tired of + N/V-ing** 對……感到厭倦

6. **look forward to + N/V-ing** 期待／盼望……(的到來)

7. **hear from sb** 接獲某人的消息／來信
   hear of... 聽過……

8. **ask sb a favor** 請某人幫忙
   = **ask a favor of sb**

A

Sunnytown High School proudly presents our yearly...

SCHOOL FAIR!

Run by the students

Open to students, teachers, and the public

Friday, June 25th, 2021

1 p.m. to 5 p.m.

Come along and buy everything from homemade cakes
and local ice cream to classic novels from our library

All money raised will go to local homeless people—
a cause that was chosen by the students themselves

Spend some money, buy nice things, and help the
homeless at Sunnytown High's School Fair!

陽光市高中獻上我們引以為傲的年度……

園遊會！

由學生主辦

開放所有師生及校外民眾蒞臨指導

2021 年六月二十五日星期五

下午一點至五點

快來買，從自製蛋糕、在地冰淇淋到
本校圖書館的經典小說，應有盡有

所有募得款項將用於本地街友 ——
由學生自行選定的目標

來陽光市高中園遊會
花點錢買好東西，幫助街友吧！

B **1.** What information is NOT given in the reading? | 文中沒有提供什麼訊息？
A. The name of the school | A. 校名
B. The prices of the items to be sold | B. 將出售物品的價格
C. When the school fair will be held | C. 校內園遊會的舉辦時間
D. Who has organized the school fair | D. 校內園遊會的主辦人

理由

問題類型：　細節題

海報第一行、第五至六行及第三行分別提及 A、C、D 項，未提及將販售物品的價格，故 B 項應為正選。

C **2.** What can you NOT buy at the school fair? | 校內園遊會中買不到什麼東西？
A. Sweet goods made at home | A. 自製甜點
B. Books provided by the school | B. 學校提供的書籍
C. Drinks provided by local firms | C. 在地商家提供的飲料
D. Cold treats from local companies | D. 來自在地商家的冰品

理由

問題類型：　細節題

根據海報第七至八行 "Come along and buy everything from homemade cakes and local ice cream to classic novels from our library"（快來買，從自製蛋糕、在地冰淇淋到本校圖書館的經典小説，應有盡有），未提及飲料，故 C 項應為正選。

D **3.** Where will the money raised from the fair go? | 園遊會中募得的款項去向為何？
A. To people who have an illness | A. 給生病的人
B. To students from poor families | B. 給來自貧困家庭的學生
C. To support the high school library | C. 用以補助高中圖書館
D. To people who don't have a home | D. 給無家可歸的人

理由

問題類型：　細節題

根據海報倒數第四行 "All money raised will go to local homeless people..."（所有募得款項將用於本地街友……），得知 D 項應為正選。

重要單字片語

1. **present** [prɪˋzɛnt] *vt.* 呈獻；頒發；提出，發表；上演 & [ˋprɛzənt] *a.* 目前的；出席的 & *n.* 禮物（= gift）

2. **yearly** [ˋjɪrlɪ] *a.* 每年的

3. **fair** [fɛr] *n.* 園遊會；市集 & *a.* 公平的

4. **homemade** [ˋhomˋmed] *a.* 自製的

5. **classic** [ˋklæsɪk] *a.* 經典的

6. **raise** [rez] *vt.* 募集；舉起；撫養（= bring up），飼養
   raise money　募款

7. **cause** [kɔz] *n.* 目標；事業；理由（= reason）& *vt.* 引起；導致

8. **organize** [ˋɔrgəˌnaɪz] *vt.* 籌劃；組織

9. **firm** [fɝm] *n.* 公司（= company）& *a.* 穩固的；堅定的

10. **treat** [trit] *n.* 美食；樂事；款待，請客 & *vt.* 招待；對待；治療

B

It's the grand opening of

FANTASTIC FURNITURE

on Saturday, August 7th, 2021

You can find our store on Main Street, next to Paulie's Pizzas

Our usual opening hours will be 9 a.m. to 6 p.m.

But on August 7th, we'll be open from 7 a.m. to 7 p.m.

And, if you're one of our first fifty customers, you'll get
10% off everything you buy!

We sell locally made tables, cabinets, and closets—
plus beds imported from Europe

Come visit us on Saturday!

盛讚傢俱行

將於 **2021** 年八月七日星期六

盛大開幕

本店在緬因街上波莉披薩店隔壁

我們一般營業時間是早上九點至下午六點

但八月七日當天將從早上七點營業至晚上七點

如果您是前五十名到場的顧客，您所購買的東西

將全部享有九折優惠！

我們販售本地製造的桌子、櫥櫃和衣櫥 ——

以及歐洲進口床

星期六前來參觀吧！

__C__ **1.** What will be different about Fantastic Furniture's first day?

　　A. It will only sell certain items.

　　B. It will close earlier than usual.

　　C. It will open for longer than usual.

　　D. It will give free pizza to customers.

盛讚傢俱行開幕首日會有什麼不同？

A. 只會販售某些品項。

B. 會比平時早打烊。

C. 營業時間會比平時長。

D. 會給顧客免費披薩。

理由

問題類型：細節題

海報前三行提及傢俱行將在八月七日開幕，而根據第五行 "Our usual opening hours will be 9 a.m. to 6 p.m."（我們一般營業時間是早上九點至下午六點）及第六行 "But on August 7th, we'll be open from 7 a.m. to 7 p.m."（但八月七日當天將從早上七點營業至晚上七點），得知開幕當日的營業時間較平時長，故 C 項應為正選。

__B__ **2.** How can shoppers save money on the opening day?

　　A. Make a post on social media

　　B. Arrive earlier than most people

　　C. Write a review on the internet

　　D. Spend a certain amount of money

顧客在開幕當天能如何省錢？

A. 在社群媒體上發文

B. 比大部分的人更早到場

C. 在網路上寫評論

D. 消費一定金額

理由

問題類型： 細節題

根據海報第七至八行 "And, if you're one of our first fifty customers, you'll get 10% off everything you buy!"（如果您是前五十名到場的顧客，您所購買的東西將全部享有九折優惠！），得知 B 項應為正選。

___C___ **3.** How are the store's beds different from its other items?

A. They are part of a special offer.

B. They are not yet available for sale.

C. They are made outside of the country.

D. They are made from a different material.

該店的床和其他商品有什麼不同？

A. 它們是特價商品的一部分。

B. 它們尚未開賣。

C. 它們是在國外製造。

D. 它們是用不同的材料製造。

理由

問題類型： 細節題

根據海報倒數第二行 "plus beds imported from Europe"（以及歐洲進口床），得知 C 項應為正選。

重要單字片語

1. **grand** [grænd] *a.* 盛大的；雄偉的；極好的，精采的（口語）

2. **opening** [ˈopənɪŋ] *n.* 開張；職缺

3. **fantastic** [fænˈtæstɪk] *a.* 極好的；幻想的

4. **furniture** [ˈfɝnɪtʃɚ] *n.* 傢俱（集合名詞，不可數）
   a piece of furniture　一件傢俱
   a lot of furniture　許多傢俱

5. **cabinet** [ˈkæbənɪt] *n.* 櫥櫃；內閣

6. **closet** [ˈklɑzɪt] *n.* 衣櫥

7. **import** [ɪmˈpɔrt] *vt.* 進口 & [ˈɪmpɔrt] *n.* 進口品

8. **post** [post] *n.*（網路）貼文；職位 & *vt.* 張貼，公布

9. **social media**　社群媒體

10. **a... amount of +** 不可數名詞
    數量……的……

A

Dear Sir,

I ordered some goods from your company, Super Prices, on December 10th. Based on your promise, all items should arrive in 48 hours. However, it is now December 17th, and they still haven't arrived. I understand that this is a busy time for your internet company, as many people are ordering presents for Christmas, but this kind of delay is not OK. I still want my goods, but I also want money off my next order.

Yours truly,
Bert Gentry

您好：

我在十二月十日那天向貴公司 Super Prices 訂購了一些商品。依貴公司的保證，所有商品應該在四十八小時內送達。然而現在已經十二月十七日了，它們卻還沒有送來。我能理解對貴網路公司來說目前是很繁忙的時刻，因為有許多人訂購聖誕節禮物，但這樣子延誤是不行的。我依然想要我的商品，但我也要求下一次訂購時給我折扣。

伯特‧簡崔　敬上

D **1.** What is the main purpose of this letter?
 A. To judge
 B. To praise
 C. To welcome
 D. To complain

這封信的主要目的是什麼？
 A. 為了評論
 B. 為了表揚
 C. 為了歡迎
 D. 為了投訴

理由

問題類型： 主旨題

信件內文前三句說明伯特跟網路公司訂購的商品未在保證的到貨期限內送達，第四句提及自己雖然能理解該公司的難處卻難以接受延誤，最後一句還要求下次訂購時享有折扣，由此可知此為一封抱怨信，故 D 項應為正選。

__B__ **2.** How many days late are the goods?

    A. Two days

    B. Five days

    C. Seven days

    D. We do not know.

這些商品運送延誤了幾天？

    A. 兩天

    B. 五天

    C. 七天

    D. 不知道。

理由

問題類型：__推論題__

信件內文第一句提及伯特於十二月十日訂貨，第二句補充網路公司保證會在四十八小時內將商品送達，得知最晚應在十二月十二日收到商品。接著第三句說他到了十二月十七日都還未收到貨，已超過保證到貨期限五天，故 B 項應為正選。

__C__ **3.** Why is it currently a busy period for Super Prices?

    A. It is the rainy season.

    B. They are having a sale.

    C. It is the holiday season.

    D. They have fired workers.

為什麼對 Super Prices 公司來說目前是繁忙時期？

    A. 現在是雨季。

    B. 它們在舉辦特賣。

    C. 現在是聖誕假期。

    D. 它們已解僱一些員工。

理由

問題類型：__細節題__

根據信件內文第四句 "I understand that this is a busy time for your internet company, as many people are ordering presents for Christmas, ..."（我能理解對貴網路公司來說目前是很繁忙的時刻，因為有許多人在訂購聖誕節禮物，……），得知 C 項應為正選。

重要單字片語

1. **goods** [gʊdz] *n.* 商品，貨物（恆用複數，不可數）

2. **promise** [ˋprɑmɪs] *n.* & *vt.* 保證，承諾

3. **off** [ɔf] *adv.* 減價，削價

4. **judge** [dʒʌdʒ] *vi.* & *vt.* 評論；批評 & *n.* 法官；裁判

5. **praise** [prez] *vt.* 表揚，稱讚 & *n.* 讚美

6. **complain** [kəmˋplen] *vi.* & *vt.* 抱怨

7. **currently** [ˋkɝəntlɪ] *adv.* 當前，目前

8. **period** [ˋpɪrɪəd] *n.* 一段時間，時期；句點

9. **fire** [faɪr] *vt.* 解僱，開除

B

To: Ms. Emma Chou

50, Shunli St., Taipei, Taiwan

Hi, Grandma!

Mom and Dad finally allowed me to go on vacation with my friends, and we're having a great time here in Florida. I'm writing this on the balcony of our hotel room. We had a fun day seeing all the people dressed up as cartoon characters and going on the rides at Disney World. Now, we're taking a rest before we go out for dinner. I'm going to have steak tonight! I can't wait to show you all my photos when I get home!

Lots of love,

Belinda

xxx

周艾瑪女士　收

臺灣臺北市順利街五十號

嗨，奶奶！

爸媽終於允許我和朋友一起去度假了，我們在佛州這裡玩得很開心。我正在我們飯店房間的陽臺上寫這張明信片。我們今天在迪士尼世界看到所有人裝扮成卡通人物，也乘坐了遊樂設施，真是好玩的一天。我們現在正在休息，然後就要出去吃晚飯了。今晚我要吃牛排！我等不及要在回家後給您看我所有的照片了！

十分愛您的，

貝琳達

給您親親

[註] 明信片最後一行 "xxx" 中的 x 為表示「親吻」的符號，在信件中常用於較親密的對象，尤用於信末，為非正式用法，但很常見。

A **1.** Who is Belinda on vacation with?
  A. Her friends
  B. Her parents
  C. Her co-workers
  D. Her grandmother

貝琳達跟誰去度假？
  A. 她朋友
  B. 她爸媽
  C. 她同事
  D. 她奶奶

理由

問題類型： 細節題

根據明信片內文開頭 "Mom and Dad finally allowed me to go on vacation with my friends, and we're having a great time here in Florida."（爸媽終於允許我和朋友一起去度假了，我們在佛州這裡玩得很開心。），得知 A 項應為正選。

C **2.** What do we know about Belinda?
  A. She does not eat meat.
  B. She is scared of flying.
  C. She stays at a hotel during the vacation.
  D. She has been to Florida with her parents before.

關於貝琳達，我們得知什麼？
  A. 她不吃肉。
  B. 她怕搭飛機。
  C. 她度假期間住在一家飯店。
  D. 她以前跟父母去過佛州。

理由

問題類型： 推論題

根據明信片內文第二句 "I'm writing this on the balcony of our hotel room."（我正在我們飯店房間的陽臺上寫這張明信片。），可推知她度假期間住在飯店，故 C 項應為正選。

C **3.** What is Belinda probably going to do next?
  A. Visit a very famous park
  B. Watch cartoons with friends
  C. Go to a restaurant for a meal
  D. Show a relative some photos

貝琳達接下來可能會做什麼？
  A. 去一座著名的公園玩
  B. 跟朋友看卡通
  C. 去餐廳吃頓飯
  D. 給親戚看些照片

理由

問題類型： 推論題

根據明信片內文第四句 "Now, we're taking a rest before we go out for dinner."（我們現在正在休息，然後就要出去吃晚飯了。），得知 C 項應為正選。

🏷 重要單字片語

1. **balcony** [ˋbælkənɪ] *n.* 陽臺（複數為 balconies）

2. **dress** [drɛs] *vt.* 給⋯⋯穿衣服（常用被動，形成下列固定用法）
   be dressed up as...　裝扮成⋯⋯

3. **ride** [raɪd] *n.* （遊樂場的）遊樂設施

4. **take a rest**　休息一下
   = **take a break**

5. **co-worker** [ˋkoˏwɝkɚ] *n.* 同事（亦可寫成 coworker）

6. **be scared of + N/V-ing**　害怕⋯⋯
   = **be afraid of + N/V-ing**

7. **probably** [ˋprɑbəblɪ] *adv.* 很可能，大概

8. **relative** [ˋrɛlətɪv] *n.* 親戚，親屬

Questionnaires & Surveys 問卷調查

A

A Great Experience with Calvin's Rent-A-Car

Please fill out the form below.

- What is your name?

  Roger Moran

- How did you find out about us?

  My friend told me about your company.

- How would you grade the service?

  ☐ **1 (very poor)**　☐ **2**　☐ **3**　☑ **4**　☐ **5 (excellent)**

- How would you grade the price?

  ☐ **1 (very poor)**　☑ **2**　☐ **3**　☐ **4**　☐ **5 (excellent)**

- How likely would you be to suggest us to your friends?

  ☐ **1 (very unlikely)**　☐ **2**　☑ **3**　☐ **4**　☐ **5 (very likely)**

卡爾文租車公司滿意體驗

請填寫下方表格。

- 您的名字是？

  羅傑・莫藍

- 您從哪裡知道我們？

  我朋友跟我提到你們公司。

- 您為本次服務打幾分？

  ☐ **1（極差）**　☐ **2**　☐ **3**　☑ **4**　☐ **5（極好）**

- 您為價格打幾分？

  ☐ **1（極差）**　☑ **2**　☐ **3**　☐ **4**　☐ **5（極好）**

- 您把我們推薦給朋友的可能性為？

  ☐ **1（極不可能）**　☐ **2**　☑ **3**　☐ **4**　☐ **5（極有可能）**

<u>A</u> **1.** What do we learn about the company on the form?

A. It rents out cars.

B. It sells used cars.

C. It is a new business.

D. It employs Roger's friend.

關於表單上的公司，我們得知哪一項？

A. 該公司出租汽車。

B. 該公司販售二手車。

C. 這是一間新公司。

D. 該公司僱用羅傑的朋友。

理由

問題類型：**推論題**

根據問卷第一句 "A Great Experience with Calvin's Rent-A-Car"（卡爾文租車公司滿意體驗）裡公司名稱中的 Rent-A-Car，可推知該公司是一家汽車出租公司，故 A 項應為正選。

<u>A</u> **2.** What does Roger think of the service at Calvin's Rent-A-Car?

A. It is good.

B. It is closer to being bad than good.

C. It requires a great deal of work.

D. It is less important than the cost.

羅傑認為卡爾文租車公司的服務如何？

A. 不錯。

B. 差強人意。

C. 需要大幅改善。

D. 其重要性不如收費。

理由

問題類型：**細節題**

羅傑在問卷中對服務（第三個問題）的評分為 4 分（僅次於「極好」），得知 A 項應為正選。

<u>B</u> **3.** Would Roger say good things to his friends about Calvin's Rent-A-Car?

A. No, certainly not.

B. The chance is 50-50.

C. Yes, without a doubt.

D. The information is not given.

羅傑會對朋友講卡爾文租車公司的好話嗎？

A. 絕對不會。

B. 機會一半一半。

C. 毫無疑問會。

D. 沒有相關訊息。

理由

問題類型：**推論題**

羅傑在問卷中對最後一個問題的評分為 3 分，得知他對卡爾文租車公司的評價為中等，故 B 項應為正選。

重要單字片語

1. **rent** [rɛnt] *vt.* 租借，出租 & *n.* 租金

2. **grade** [gred] *vt.* 為……評分；將……分等級 & *n.* 等級；成績（常用複數）

3. **likely** [ˈlaɪklɪ] *a.* 有可能的 & *adv.* 可能
   It is likely that + S + V   很可能……
   = S + be likely to V

4. **employ** [ɪmˈplɔɪ] *vt.* 僱用；運用

5. **think of...**   認為……；想到……

6. **require** [rɪˈkwaɪr] *vt.* 需要；要求
   be required to V   必須做……

7. **a great deal of + 不可數名詞**
   大量的……

8. **certainly** [ˈsɝtn̩lɪ] *adv.* 當然（= of course）

9. **without (a) doubt**   毫無疑問

B

Why are you leaving?

1. What is your name?
   Melissa Barr

2. How long have you worked for the company?
   Over nine years

3. Which department did you work in?
   I first worked in buying, and then in marketing.

4. Why did you decide to leave the company?
   I feel like I need to test myself in a different field.

5. What was the best part about working for the company?
   Working with lots of great people in different departments

6. What was the worst part about working for the company?
   The managers would not change to modern working practices.

您為何要離職？

1. 您的名字是？
   梅麗莎・巴爾

2. 您在本公司服務多久了？
   超過九年

3. 您任職於哪一個部門？
   我剛開始在採購部，後來到行銷部。

4. 您為什麼決定離職？
   我覺得需要在不同的領域中自我挑戰。

5. 您認為在本公司任職最喜歡的一點是什麼？
   和不同部門的許多好人共事

6. 您認為在本公司任職最不喜歡的一點是什麼？
   經理人不願改成現代化的工作方式。

<u>A</u> **1.** Why has Melissa filled out this form?

A. She has quit her job.

B. She is applying for a job.

C. She is borrowing some money.

D. She has bought something new.

梅麗莎為什麼填寫這份表格？

A. 她辭職了。

B. 她要應徵工作。

C. 她要借錢。

D. 她買了新東西。

理由

問題類型： 推論題

根據問卷標題 Why are you leaving?（您為何要離職？）、第四個問題 "Why did you decide to leave the company?"（您為什麼決定離職？）及其他問題，可推知這份問卷為離職前填寫用，故 A 項應為正選。

<u>C</u> **2.** What is NOT true about Melissa?

A. She wants to change to a new career.

B. She worked in two different departments.

C. She was a manager in the buying department.

D. She worked at the company for nearly ten years.

關於梅麗莎的敘述哪一項不正確？

A. 她想轉換跑道。

B. 她曾任職於兩個不同部門。

C. 她曾任採購部門經理。

D. 她曾在這家公司任職近十年。

CH 1

問題類型： 細節題

問卷第四、第三及第二個問題分別提及 A、B、D 項，整份問卷未提及梅麗莎曾任採購部門經理，故 C 項敘述錯誤，應為正選。

D **3.** What does Melissa consider a negative part of working for the company?

A. There was too little space.

B. There were too many tests.

C. The people were not friendly.

D. The managers were too traditional.

梅麗莎認為任職於該公司的一項缺點是什麼？

A. 空間太小。

B. 考核太多。

C. 同事不友善。

D. 經理人太傳統。

理由

問題類型： 細節題

針對問卷第六個問題 "What was the worst part about working for the company?"（您認為在本公司任職最不喜歡的一點是什麼？），梅麗莎回答 "The managers would not change to modern working practices."（經理人不願改成現代化的工作方式。），故 D 項應為正選。

🔖 重要單字片語

1. **department** [dɪˋpɑrtmənt] *n.* 部門；（學校的）系

2. **manager** [ˋmænɪdʒɚ] *n.* 經理

3. **quit** [kwɪt] *vt.* 辭（職）；停止；戒除 & *vi.* 辭職（三態同形）

4. **apply for...** 應徵……；申請……

5. **career** [kəˋrɪr] *n.* 職業（尤指終身職業）

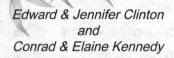

A

Edward & Jennifer Clinton
and
Conrad & Elaine Kennedy

invite you to attend
the wedding of their children

Gareth Clinton
and
Sophia Kennedy

on Saturday, June 11th, 2022

The service will take place at 1 p.m. at
New Church, Forest Road, Darlington

The wedding party will follow at 3 p.m. at
Bartle Hall, Wood Road, Darlington

Gareth and Sophia ask that you do not bring gifts

Formal clothes are required

愛德華與珍妮佛・柯林頓
偕
康拉德與伊蓮・甘迺迪

敬邀蒞臨其愛子及愛女

加雷斯・柯林頓
與
蘇菲亞・甘迺迪

於 2022 年六月十一日星期六舉行之婚禮

婚禮儀式將於下午一點在達林頓鎮森林路之新教堂舉行

喜宴隨後於下午三點在達林頓鎮樹林路之巴托廳舉行

加雷斯與蘇菲亞婉謝禮金禮物

請穿著正式服裝

__D__ **1.** Who will Edward Clinton become on the day of the wedding?

A. Elaine's husband

B. Gareth's father-in-law

C. Jennifer's ex-husband

D. Sophia's father-in-law

愛德華・柯林頓在婚禮當天會變為什麼身分？

A. 伊蓮的丈夫

B. 加雷斯的岳父

C. 珍妮佛的前夫

D. 蘇菲亞的公公

理由

問題類型： 推論題

本喜帖前半部說明 Clinton（柯林頓）及 Kennedy（甘迺迪）兩對夫婦邀請親友蒞臨其子女的婚禮，接著提到新郎為 Gareth Clinton（加雷斯・柯林頓）、新娘為 Sophia Kennedy（蘇菲亞・甘迺迪）。根據上述姓氏及相關身分，得知 Edward Clinton（愛德華・柯林頓）為新郎的父親，婚禮過後即成為新娘的公公，故 D 項應為正選。

__B__ **2.** What will happen at 3 p.m.?

A. The guests will arrive at the church.

B. The guests will get ready to have a big meal.

C. Gareth and Sophia will start to open their gifts.

D. Gareth and Sophia will become husband and wife.

下午三點會發生什麼事？

A. 賓客會抵達教堂。

B. 賓客會準備享用大餐。

C. 加雷斯與蘇菲亞會開始拆禮物。

D. 加雷斯與蘇菲亞會成為夫妻。

理由

問題類型： 細節題

根據本喜帖倒數第三段 "The wedding party will follow at 3 p.m. at Bartle Hall, Wood Road, Darlington"（喜宴隨後於下午三點在達林頓鎮樹林路之巴托廳舉行），得知 B 項應為正選。

__A__ **3.** Based on the invitation, which of the following is true?

A. The wedding will be on the weekend.

B. The hosts will only accept small gifts.

C. The guests aren't required to wear formal clothes.

D. The guests are advised to have lunch before the wedding.

根據本喜帖，下列哪一項是正確的？

A. 婚禮會在週末舉行。

B. 主人只會收小禮物。

C. 未要求賓客穿正式服裝。

D. 建議賓客在婚禮前要吃午餐。

理由

問題類型：細節題

根據本喜帖第四段 "on Saturday, June 11th, 2022"（於 2022 年六月十一日星期六舉行），
得知 A 項應為正選。

 重要單字片語

1. **invite** [ɪnˈvaɪt] *vt.* 邀請
   invite sb to V　邀請某人做……
   invite sb to + 地方　邀請某人去某地

2. **attend** [əˈtɛnd] *vt.* 參加

3. **wedding** [ˈwɛdɪŋ] *n.* 婚禮

4. **service** [ˈsɝvɪs] *n.* 宗教儀式；服務

5. **formal** [ˈfɔrml̩] *a.* 正式的

6. **-in-law**　　姻親關係的……
   father-in-law　岳父；公公
   mother-in-law　岳母；婆婆

7. **ex-** [ɛks] *prefix* 前任的，以前的
   ex-husband　前夫
   ex-wife　前妻

B

Dear Hilary,

I was really sorry to hear about your accident. At your age, you really shouldn't be climbing so high, though! You should have hired someone to paint the house for you! You were so lucky that your grandson happened to drive by your house and saw you lying on the ground. I hope your leg and arm get better soon. I will come to visit you in the hospital as soon as I get back from my summer trip next week. I'm sorry I can't visit you sooner.

Get well soon!

Dennis

親愛的希拉蕊：

聽到妳出意外我很難過。不過以妳這個年紀真不該爬那麼高！妳應該要僱人幫妳粉刷房子才對！妳真幸運妳的孫子剛好開車經過看到妳躺在地上。希望妳的腿和手臂趕快復元。我下禮拜暑假旅遊一回來就去醫院看妳。很抱歉沒法更早過去看妳。

祝妳早日康復！

丹尼斯

<u>A</u> **1.** What happened to Hilary?
A. She fell while painting.
B. She caught a serious illness.
C. She was hurt in a car accident.
D. She got lost climbing a mountain.

希拉蕊發生了什麼事？
A. 她在粉刷時摔到地上。
B. 她生了一場重病。
C. 她發生車禍受傷。
D. 她登山時迷路。

理由

問題類型： 推論題
本慰問卡一開始丹尼斯提及希拉蕊出意外，並認為她不該爬高，第三句意味希拉蕊自己粉刷房子太勉強，第四句敘述她被發現時人躺在地上，可推論希拉蕊應是試圖自己粉刷房子時不慎摔落地面受傷，故 A 項應為正選。

B **2.** Why does Dennis talk about Hilary's grandson?

    A. The grandson is a painter.

    B. The grandson saved Hilary.

    C. The grandson caused an accident.

    D. The grandson thinks Hilary is lying.

丹尼斯為何提到希拉蕊的孫子？

A. 孫子是畫家。

B. 孫子救了希拉蕊。

C. 孫子導致意外。

D. 孫子認為希拉蕊說謊。

理由

問題類型： 細節題

根據本慰問卡第四句 "You were so lucky that your grandson happened to drive by your house and saw you lying on the ground."（妳真幸運妳的孫子剛好開車經過看到妳躺在地上。），得知 B 項應為正選。

A **3.** Why hasn't Dennis visited Hilary yet?

    A. He is on vacation.

    B. His car broke down.

    C. He hurt his leg and arm.

    D. He is in another hospital.

丹尼斯為什麼還沒去探視希拉蕊？

A. 他正在度假。

B. 他的車子拋錨。

C. 他的腿和手臂受傷。

D. 他住在別家醫院。

理由

問題類型： 細節題

根據本慰問卡倒數兩句 "I will come to visit you in the hospital as soon as I get back from my summer trip next week. I'm sorry I can't visit you sooner."（我下禮拜暑假旅遊一回來就去醫院看妳。很抱歉沒法更早過去看妳。），得知 A 項應為正選。

🔖 重要單字片語

1. climb [klaɪm] *vi.* & *vt.* 攀爬

2. lie [laɪ] *vi.* 躺（三態為：lie, lay [le], lain [len]，現在分詞為 lying）

3. (be) on vacation （正在）度 / 休假

4. sth break down （車輛）拋錨；（機器）故障

    sb break down （人）崩潰

Price Lists & Menus 價目表與菜單

A

Carol's Cleaning Company Price List	
Service	**Price**
Kitchen – standard clean	$40 every hour
Kitchen – heavy clean	$60 every hour
Bathroom – standard clean	$50 every hour
Bathroom – heavy clean	$70 every hour
One-bedroom apartment	$90 every hour
Two-bedroom apartment	$90 every hour
Three-bedroom apartment	$90 every hour
Small house	$100 every hour
Large house	$120 every hour
Garage	$40 every hour

Please note:

Carol's Cleaning Company will refuse to clean your home if there is any danger to our workers.

卡蘿清潔公司 價目表	
服務項目	**價格**
廚房 —— 標準清潔	每小時四十美元
廚房 —— 深度清潔	每小時六十美元
浴室 —— 標準清潔	每小時五十美元
浴室 —— 深度清潔	每小時七十美元
一房公寓	每小時九十美元
兩房公寓	每小時九十美元
三房公寓	每小時九十美元
小型獨棟	每小時一百美元
大型獨棟	每小時一百二十美元
車庫	每小時四十美元

請注意：

若打掃您的房屋會為我們的員工帶來危險，卡蘿清潔公司將拒絕清掃。

A **1.** Which is the most expensive service that Carol's Cleaning Company provides?
   A. A clean of a big house
   B. A heavy clean of a kitchen
   C. A clean of a large apartment
   D. A heavy clean of a bathroom

卡蘿清潔公司所提供的服務中，價格最高的是哪一項？
   A. 打掃大型獨棟
   B. 深度打掃廚房
   C. 打掃大型公寓
   D. 深度打掃浴室

理由

問題類型： **細節題**

根據價目表倒數第二列，清掃大型獨棟的價格為每小時一百二十美元，為所有服務中最高，故 A 項應為正選。

A **2.** What can we learn about the company?
   A. It charges by the hour.
   B. It employs only one cleaner.
   C. It cleans homes and businesses.
   D. It has been around for ten years.

關於這家公司，我們可以得知哪一項？
   A. 它以小時計費。
   B. 它只僱有一位清潔員。
   C. 它打掃住宅與公司。
   D. 它已成立十年。

理由

問題類型： **細節題**

根據價目表右欄，得知這家公司的打掃計價單位為小時，故 A 項應為正選。

C **3.** Laura wants to use the services of Carol's Cleaning Company. There are two bathrooms that require a heavy clean in her house. How much would it cost her every hour?
   A. $100
   B. $120
   C. $140
   A. $160

蘿拉想使用卡蘿清潔公司的服務。她住的房子有兩間浴室需要深度清潔。她每小時要花多少錢？
   A. 一百美元
   B. 一百二十美元
   C. 一百四十美元
   D. 一百六十美元

理由

問題類型： **情境題**

根據價目表第六列，浴室深度清潔為每小時七十美元，蘿拉的房子有兩間浴室需要打掃，共需一百四十美元，故 C 項應為正選。

CH
1

重要單字片語

1. **apartment** [əˈpɑrtmənt] *n.* 公寓（美式用法）

2. **garage** [gəˈrɑʒ] *n.* 車庫

3. **refuse** [rɪˈfjuz] *vi. & vt.* 拒絕
   refuse to V　　拒絕做……

4. **danger** [ˈdendʒɚ] *n.* 危險
   be in danger of + N/V-ing
   有……的危險

B

Mia's Coffee Shop
❧ Menu ❧

❋ First Course

Garden Salad	$8
Ham Salad	$10
Bread & Butter	$5

❋ Soup

Tomato Soup	$7.50
French Onion Soup	$9.50
Beef Soup	$11.50

❋ Main Course

Egg on Toast	$12
Fried Chicken	$14.50
Turkey Sandwich	$15.50

❋ Dessert

Chocolate Cake	$10
Apple Pie	$11.50
Ice Cream	$7.50

❋ Drink

Hot Black Coffee	$4.50
Hot White Coffee	$5.50
Iced Green Tea	$5

Please note: A service charge of 10% will be added to your bill.

米亞咖啡廳

❧ 菜單 ❧

❀ 前菜		❀ 甜點	
花園沙拉	8 美元	巧克力蛋糕	10 美元
火腿沙拉	10 美元	蘋果派	11.50 美元
麵包附奶油	5 美元	冰淇淋	7.50 美元

❀ 湯		❀ 飲料	
番茄湯	7.50 美元	熱黑咖啡	4.50 美元
法式洋蔥湯	9.50 美元	熱白咖啡	5.50 美元
牛肉湯	11.50 美元	冰綠茶	5 美元

❀ 主菜	
蛋吐司	12 美元
炸雞	14.50 美元
火雞肉三明治	15.50 美元

請注意：帳單會加收 10% 服務費。

A **1.** What is NOT true about Mia's Coffee Shop?

    A. It offers three kinds of hot drinks.

    B. It offers more than one type of salad.

    C. It offers one soup that includes meat.

    D. It offers more than one choice of dessert.

關於米亞咖啡廳，哪一項敘述不正確？

    A. 它提供三種熱飲。

    C. 它提供的沙拉不只一種。

    D. 它提供一種含有肉類的湯。

    B. 它提供的甜點選擇不只一種。

理由

問題類型：細節題

根據菜單中的飲料欄位，熱飲只有 Hot Black Coffee（熱黑咖啡）和 Hot White Coffee（熱白咖啡），得知 A 項敘述錯誤，故應為正選。

CH 1

__D__ **2.** What does the message at the bottom of the menu mean?

A. The coffee shop will only accept cash.

B. The coffee shop would like you to tip the waiters.

C. The coffee shop would welcome any notes or comments.

D. The coffee shop will include another charge on your bill.

菜單最底下的訊息是什麼意思？

A. 咖啡廳只收現金。

B. 咖啡廳希望你給服務生小費。

C. 咖啡廳歡迎任何想法和建議。

D. 咖啡廳將在帳單中加上另一筆費用。

理由

問題類型：__推論題__

菜單最下方的敘述 "Please note: A service charge of 10% will be added to your bill."（請注意：帳單會加收 10% 服務費。）表示消費金額會包含服務費，故 D 項應為正選。

__C__ **3.** Todd buys a ham salad and a chocolate cake. What is the total bill?

A. $18

B. $20

C. $22

D. $21.5

陶德買了一份火腿沙拉和一塊巧克力蛋糕。帳單總共多少錢？

A. 18 美元

B. 20 美元

C. 22 美元

D. 21.5 美元

理由

問題類型：__情境題__

根據菜單，ham salad（火腿沙拉）和 chocolate cake（巧克力蛋糕）的價格都是 10 美元，共 20 美元，再加 10% 的服務費 2 元，因此共須付 22 元，故 C 項應為正選。

🏷 **重要單字片語**

1. **course** [kɔrs] *n.* 一道菜；課程；路徑
   a main course　主菜

2. **ham** [hæm] *n.* 火腿

3. **onion** [ˋʌnjən] *n.* 洋蔥

4. **toast** [tost] *n.* 吐司（不可數）

5. **turkey** [ˋtɝkɪ] *n.* 火雞肉；火雞

6. **bill** [bɪl] *n.* 帳單；紙鈔；法案

7. **cash** [kæʃ] *n.* 現金 & *vt.* （將支票等）兌現

8. **tip** [tɪp] *vt.* 給小費 & *n.* 小費；尖端；秘訣

9. **comment** [ˋkɑmɛnt] *n.* 評語，意見，批評 & *vi.* 評論（均與介詞 on 並用）
   make a comment on...　對……做評論或發表意見
   = comment on...

A

Bobby,

I hope you're looking forward to the trip! I should arrive at the camping ground at 10 a.m. on Friday. As you'll arrive later than me, I'm leaving you a map showing you how to get there. Park your car in the parking lot at the bottom of Great Hill, and set off walking. Make sure you pick the safest path!

Ronald

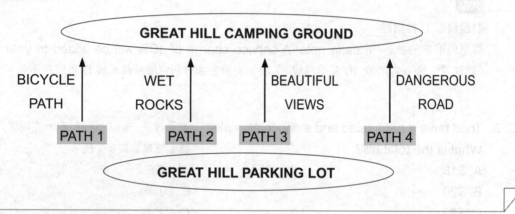

巴比：

希望你是很期待這次旅遊的！我應該會在星期五早上十點抵達露營場地。由於你會比我晚抵達，所以我留一張地圖給你告訴你怎麼過去。把你的車停在大山丘山腳下的停車場，然後開始步行。一定要選最安全的路線喔！

羅納德

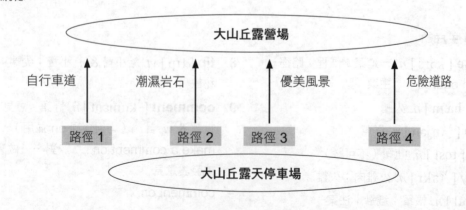

CH
1

__B__ **1.** Why is Ronald leaving a map for Bobby?

 A. Ronald is playing a joke on Bobby.

 B. Bobby is not traveling with Ronald.

 C. Bobby has a poor sense of direction.

 D. Ronald is worried Bobby will be late.

羅納德為何留一張地圖給巴比？

 A. 羅納德在開巴比的玩笑。

 B. 巴比沒有跟羅納德一起過去。

 C. 巴比的方向感很差。

 D. 羅納德擔心巴比會遲到。

理由

問題類型：細節題

根據本文第三句 "As you'll arrive later than me, I'm leaving you a map showing you how to get there."（由於你會比我晚抵達，所以我留一張地圖給你告訴你怎麼過去。），得知 B 項應為正選。

__D__ **2.** How will Ronald travel to the parking lot?

 A. By car

 B. On foot

 C. By bicycle

 D. We do not know.

羅納德會怎麼去停車場？

 A. 開車

 B. 走路

 C. 騎自行車

 D. 不知道。

理由

問題類型：推論題

本文從頭到尾都是羅納德在告訴巴比如何到達露營場地，並未提及自己要如何去停車場，故 D 項應為正選。

__C__ **3.** Which path will Bobby probably take to the camping ground?

 A. Path 1

 B. Path 2

 C. Path 3

 D. Path 4

巴比可能會挑選哪條路徑去露營場地？

 A. 路徑 1

 B. 路徑 2

 C. 路徑 3

 D. 路徑 4

理由

問題類型：推論題

根據本文倒數第二句 "Park your car in the parking lot at the bottom of Great Hill, and set off walking."（把你的車停在大山丘山腳下的停車場，然後開始步行。），得知巴比會走路過去，A 項路徑 1 為 bicycle bath（自行車道）不可選。另根據本文最後一句 "Make sure you pick the safest path!"（一定要選最安全的路線喔！），得知巴比應走安全的路，B 項路徑 2 為 wet rocks（潮濕岩石）、D 項路徑 4 為 dangerous road（危險道路），兩者都不安全所以皆不可選，故 C 項應為正選。

🔖 重要單字片語

1. **camping** [ˈkæmpɪŋ] *n.* 露營
2. **ground** [graʊnd] *n.* 場地；地面
3. **bottom** [ˈbɑtəm] *n.* 底部，下端
4. **set off (for / to + 地方)**
   出發／啟程（前往某地）

5. **a sense of...**   ⋯⋯感
   a sense of direction   方向感
6. **on foot**   走路，步行

B

Dear students,

Please see below the floor plan of the school.

CLEANING ROOM	GIRLS' RESTROOM	BOYS' RESTROOM		LUNCH ROOM	PRINCIPAL'S OFFICE
ENGLISH ROOM	HISTORY ROOM	GEOGRAPHY ROOM	MAIN HALL	BIOLOGY ROOM	PHYSICS ROOM
MATH ROOM	ART ROOM	COMPUTER ROOM		GYM	

Please note: The gym will be closed for repair work from February 1st to February 10th.
Gym classes will move to the main hall. Any events that were to take place in the main
hall during this time will be canceled.

各位同學好：

請看以下的學校平面圖。

掃具間	女廁	男廁		學校餐廳	校長室
英語教室	歷史教室	地理教室	大廳	生物教室	物理教室
數學教室	美術教室	電腦教室		體育館	

請注意：體育館將於二月一日至十日關閉進行維修。體育課會換到大廳上課。這段期間原本將在
大廳舉行的任何活動將被取消。

CH 1

B **1.** Which of the following is true about the school?
    A. The art room is next to the history room.
    B. The English room is across from the math room.
    C. The geography room is next to the girls' restroom.
    D. The cleaning room is across from the computer room.

關於這間學校,下列哪一項是正確的?
A. 美術教室在歷史教室隔壁。
B. 英語教室在數學教室對面。
C. 地理教室在女廁隔壁。
D. 掃具間在電腦教室對面。

理由

問題類型: **細節題**

根據本平面圖得知英語教室及數學教室均位於學校最左側且彼此位置相對,故 B 項應為正選。

A **2.** The school planned to hold a music show in the main hall on February 5th. What will happen to that show?
    A. It will not take place.
    B. It will take place in the gym.
    C. It will take place in a new hall.
    D. It will be changed to February 10th.

校方打算於二月五日在大廳舉辦音樂表演。這場表演會怎麼樣?
A. 不會舉行。
B. 會在體育館舉行。
C. 會在新的大廳舉行。
D. 會改到二月十日。

理由

問題類型: **情境題**

根據本平面圖下方備註第一句 "The gym will be closed for repair work from February 1st to February 10th."(體育館將於二月一日至十日關閉進行維修。)及第三句 "Any events that were to take place in the main hall during this time will be canceled."(這段期間原本將在大廳舉行的任何活動將被取消。),得知這場音樂表演會被取消,故 A 項應為正選。

C **3.** Jill is in one of the classrooms. The classroom is between two other classrooms, and there are no restrooms across from her classroom. Which classroom is she in?
    A. The English room
    B. The biology room
    C. The art room
    D. The geography room

吉兒在某間教室。該教室在另外兩間教室中間,而且對面沒有廁所。她在哪一間教室?
A. 英語教室
B. 生物教室
C. 美術教室
D. 地理教室

理由

問題類型：<u>情境題</u>

根據本平面圖得知大廳左側的每一列有三個房間，選項中只有 C 項 **The art room**（美術教室）位於大廳左側其中一排的中間且對面沒有廁所，故 C 項應為正選。

🏷 重要單字片語

1. **a floor plan** 樓層平面圖
2. **restroom** [ˋrɛstͺrum] n. 公廁，洗手間
3. **principal** [ˋprɪnsəpḷ] n.（公立學校的）校長
4. **geography** [dʒɪˋɑgrəfɪ] n. 地理（學）
5. **biology** [baɪˋɑlədʒɪ] n. 生物學
6. **physics** [ˋfɪzɪks] n. 物理學
7. **take place** （事件）舉行；發生
8. **cancel** [ˋkænsḷ] vt. 取消
9. **across from...** 在⋯⋯的對面

多文本閱讀

詳解

MIXED WEATHER FOR WEEK AHEAD

By Andreas Jones

Weather Reporter

The mixed weather we've been experiencing will continue into next week. You will need to have everything from sun hats to rain jackets at the ready! Monday and Tuesday will be very hot, with high temperatures of 29ºC. A cold front means the temperature will drop to 19ºC on Wednesday, but the weather will still be dry. The heavy rain will arrive on Thursday, and the temperature will drop by a further three to four degrees. At least there won't be any snow next week!

Dear Diary,

I was really looking forward to our school trip to the farm today. I wanted to see the cows and feed the lambs. However, our teacher told us that we couldn't go because of the bad weather. I don't know why we couldn't just take our umbrellas and carry on with the trip. We might get a bit wet, but that's no big deal. When it was canceled, I thought we might at least do something fun in class—play games or watch a movie. But we just did our usual subjects. I hate bad weather!

Zosia

未來一週天氣多變

氣象預報員

安迪瑞亞斯・瓊斯

最近的多變天氣將持續到下週。您將需要準備好包括遮陽帽和雨衣等一切物品！星期一和星期二會很熱，高溫達攝氏二十九度。星期三有一道冷鋒來襲，意味著氣溫將降至攝氏十九度，但天氣依然乾燥。星期四將降下豪雨，氣溫會再降三到四度。至少下週不會下雪！

> 親愛的日記：
>
> 我原本真的很期待今天的農場校外教學。我想看牛群也想餵小羊。但我們老師說因為天氣不好所以不能去了。我不懂為什麼我們不能帶雨傘然後照樣去校外教學。我們可能會稍微淋濕，但是那也沒什麼大不了。校外教學取消後，我以為我們至少可以在課堂上做點好玩的事 —— 玩遊戲或是看部電影。但是我們只是像平常一樣上正課。我討厭壞天氣！
>
> 柔西亞

__C__ 1. What is NOT true about the week's weather?
A. Tuesday will be as hot as Monday.
B. Thursday will be colder than Tuesday.
C. Wednesday will be colder than Thursday.
D. Monday will be warmer than Wednesday.

關於該週天氣的敘述哪一項不正確？
A. 星期二會像星期一一樣熱。
B. 星期四會比星期二冷。
C. 星期三會比星期四冷。
D. 星期一會比星期三暖和。

理由

問題類型：細節題

根據天氣預報第四句 "...the temperature will drop to 19℃ on Wednesday..."（星期三……氣溫將降至攝氏十九度……）及第五句 "...on Thursday, and the temperature will drop by a further three to four degrees."（星期四……，氣溫會再降三到四度。），得知 C 項敘述錯誤，故應為正選。

__D__ 2. How did Zosia feel when she wrote her diary?
A. She was excited to have seen some animals.
B. She was looking forward to a coming activity.
C. She was embarrassed to get all wet in the rain.
D. She was sad about something that didn't happen.

柔西亞寫日記時心情如何？
A. 她看到了一些動物很興奮。
B. 她很期待某個即將到來的活動。
C. 她在雨中全身濕透很尷尬。
D. 她對於某件沒發生的事感到難過。

理由

問題類型：推論題

根據日記內文倒數三句 "When it was canceled, I thought we might at least do something fun in class—play games or watch a movie. But we just did our usual subjects. I hate bad weather!"（校外教學取消後，我以為我們至少可以在課堂上做點好玩的事 ── 玩遊戲或是看部電影。但是我們只是像平常一樣上正課。我討厭壞天氣！），可推知柔西亞寫日記時既沮喪又失望，故 D 項應為正選。

D 3. On which day did Zosia write her diary?　　柔西亞是在哪一天寫日記？

　　A. Monday　　　　　　　　　　　　A. 星期一

　　B. Tuesday　　　　　　　　　　　　B. 星期二

　　C. Wednesday　　　　　　　　　　C. 星期三

　　D. Thursday　　　　　　　　　　　D. 星期四

理由

問題類型：推論題

柔西亞在日記內文第一句提及今天原本要去校外教學，第三句敘述老師說因為天氣不好因此取消校外教學行程，第四句表示她認為可以帶著雨傘去校外教學，而根據天氣預報第五句 "The heavy rain will arrive on Thursday..."（星期四將降下豪雨⋯⋯），得知柔西亞寫日記當天是星期四，故 D 項應為正選。

🏷 重要單字片語

1. **ahead** [əˋhɛd] *adv.* 未來，今後；在前面，在前方

2. **continue** [kənˋtɪnju] *vi. & vt.* 繼續；持續

　　continue + V-ing　　繼續做⋯⋯

　= continue to V

　= go on + V-ing

3. **at the ready**　　準備好；可隨時使用

4. **temperature** [ˋtɛmp(ə)rətʃɚ] *n.* 溫度；體溫

5. **a cold front**　　冷鋒

6. **drop** [drɑp] *vi.* 下降 & *vt.* 使掉落 & *n.*（一）滴；下降

7. **further** [ˋfɝðɚ] *a.* 更進一步的，更多的 & *adv.* 更進一步

8. **degree** [dɪˋgri] *n.* 度（數）；程度，等級；學位

9. **at least**　　至少

10. **look forward to + N/V-ing**
　　期待⋯⋯

11. **feed** [fid] *vt.* 餵食 & *vi.* 以⋯⋯為食物（與介詞 on 並用）

12. **carry on with...**　　繼續／照常做⋯⋯

13. **be no big deal**　　沒什麼大不了

14. **cancel** [ˋkænsl̩] *vt.* 取消（= call off）

HELP WANTED!

We are a busy restaurant in the center of Manhattan, and we're looking for a cook to join our kitchen team. We require that you:

- Have attended cooking school in the US
- Have worked in a kitchen before
- Are able to work lunch and dinner times
- Are able to deal with a busy kitchen environment

You will be paid $20 an hour, and you will get two days off each week.

For more information and to apply, please visit:

www.rheasrestaurant.com

RHEA'S RESTAURANT
JOB FORM

Date: *07.08.2021*

Name	*Anthony Ramsay*
Email	*tonyram@coldmail.com*
Education	*I studied for three years at Cumbria Cooking School in the UK.*
Current Position	*Cook at Morgana's Restaurant, New York*
Date Available	*August 1st, 2021*
Times Available	*(Please underline)* Breakfast <u>Lunch</u> <u>Dinner</u>
Personal Comment	*I am an excellent cook with experience in another busy New York restaurant. Although I like my current job, I want to push myself further, make new dishes, and work with new people. I am available for an interview right away.*

徵廚師

曼哈頓中心地段人氣餐廳徵求廚師一名加入廚房團隊。資格：

- 上過美國的烹飪學校
- 曾在廚房工作過
- 能夠在午餐和晚餐時間上班
- 能夠應付忙碌的廚房環境

待遇為時薪二十美元，週休二日。

欲知更多資訊及應徵方式，請至：

www.rheasrestaurant.com

芮雅餐廳
求職申請表

日期： *2021 年七月八日*

姓名	*安東尼‧雷姆西*
電子郵件地址	*tonyram@coldmail.com*
學歷	*我曾在英國坎布里亞郡烹飪學校就讀三年。*
目前職位	*在紐約的摩加納餐廳擔任廚師*
可上班日期	*2021 年八月一日*
可上班時段	*（請在底下劃線）* *早餐　午餐　晚餐*
附帶說明	*我是優秀的廚師，曾在紐約另一家忙碌的餐廳工作。雖然我喜歡現在的工作，但我想督促自己進步、學做新菜、和不同的人一起工作。我可以立即進行面試。*

C 1. What is the purpose of the first reading?

A. To find someone to cook for a school

B. To search for a cook who stole money

C. To find someone to work in a restaurant

D. To search for someone to clean a kitchen

第一篇閱讀文本的目的是什麼？

A. 找人幫某學校煮飯

B. 搜尋偷錢的廚師

C. 找人來某餐廳上班

D. 找人打掃廚房

理由

問題類型：　主旨題

根據徵才廣告內文第一句 "We are a busy restaurant in the center of Manhattan, and we're looking for a cook to join our kitchen team."（曼哈頓中心地段人氣餐廳徵求廚師一名加入廚房團隊。），得知 C 項應為正選。

A 2. What do we know about Anthony?

A. He has career goals.

B. He is married to Morgana.

C. He wants to earn more money.

D. He doesn't like working weekends.

關於安東尼，我們得知哪一項？

A. 他有職涯目標。

B. 他娶了摩加納。

C. 他想賺更多錢。

D. 他不喜歡在週末工作。

理由

問題類型：　推論題

根據求職表最後一列 Personal Comment（附帶說明）第二句 "Although I like my current job, I want to push myself further, make new dishes, and work with new people."（雖然我喜歡現在的工作，但我想督促自己進步、學做新菜、和不同的人一起工作。），可推知安東尼對於職涯有自己的目標，得知 A 項應為正選。

C 3. Why might Anthony NOT get the job at the restaurant?

A. He cannot work at breakfast time.

B. He cannot start work straight away.

C. He didn't go to an American school.

D. He doesn't have enough experience.

為什麼安東尼可能無法得到這家餐廳的工作？

A. 他無法在早餐時間上班。

B. 他無法馬上開始上班。

C. 他沒有上過美國的學校。

D. 他沒有足夠的經驗。

理由

問題類型：　多文本整合題

根據徵才廣告資格要求的第一點 Have attended cooking school in the US（上過美國的烹飪學校）及求職表內容第三列 Education（學歷）的敘述 "I studied for three years at Cumbria Cooking School in the UK."（我曾在英國坎布里亞郡烹飪學校就讀三年。），得知安東尼的學歷不符餐廳該項要求資格，故 C 項應為正選。

重要單字片語

1. **look for...**　尋找……

2. **deal with...**　處理 / 應付……

3. **environment** [ɪnˋvaɪrənmənt] *n.*
   環境；周圍狀況

4. **information** [͵ɪnfɚˋmeʃən] *n.* 消息，
   資料（不可數，有時縮寫成 info [ˋɪnfo]）

5. **education** [͵ɛdʒʊˋkeʃən] *n.* 教育；學歷

6. **current** [ˋkɝnt] *a.* 目前的

7. **position** [pəˋzɪʃən] *n.* 職位；位置

8. **available** [əˋveləbḷ] *a.* 有空的；可獲得的

9. **underline** [͵ʌndɚˋlaɪn] *vt.* 在……下面
   劃線；凸顯

10. **interview** [ˋɪntɚ͵vju] *n. & vt.* 面試；
    訪問

11. **right away**　立即，馬上
    = **straight away**

TV GUIDE

Time	Channel	Program	Information
	\multicolumn{3}{} Saturday, August 21st		

Time	Channel	Program	Information
8 p.m.	Channel 10	*Fly Away Today*	A show following one man's travels around the world
	Channel ABC	Movie: *Sooner or Later*	A will-they-won't-they love story about a couple from different countries
10 p.m.	Channel 10	*Music Is My Life*	The beautiful story of a child's love of music
	Channel ABC	Movie: *One of Us Must Know*	This ghost movie will make you feel scared and keep you up at night!

CH
2

Daisy Where are you? It's almost 7:30.   7:27 p.m.

7:31 p.m.   Sorry. The team and I were discussing the game.   **Joe**

Daisy When will you be home?   7:32 p.m.
The movie starts at 8:00.

7:36 p.m.   Probably not till 8:15. Sorry I can't make it. How about the one at 10:00? I can watch that with you.   **Joe**

Daisy I don't want to be frightened and have bad dreams! I   7:37 p.m.
want to watch the one we agreed on: the love story!

7:45 p.m.   OK, whatever you want.   **Joe**

電視節目表

八月二十一日 星期六			
時間	頻道	節目	內容
晚上八點	十號頻道	《萬里翱遊》	這個節目跟拍某個男人的世界之旅
	ABC 頻道	電影：《緣來擋不住》	一對不同國籍的戀人分分合合的愛情故事
晚上十點	十號頻道	《音樂人生》	一個熱愛音樂的孩子的美麗故事
	ABC 頻道	電影：《搞鬼你或我》	這部鬼片會讓你害怕到整晚睡不著！

黛西　你在哪裡？快七點半了耶。　　晚上七點二十七分

晚上七點三十一分　　抱歉，我跟隊友在檢討比賽。　喬

黛西　你什麼時候會到家？電影　晚上七點三十二分
八點開始喔。

晚上七點三十六分　　可能要八點十五分以後。抱歉我趕不及了。
十點那部電影怎麼樣？我可以跟妳一起看。　喬

黛西　我不想被嚇到做惡夢！我要看我們講好的　晚上七點三十七分
那一部：愛情故事！

晚上七點四十五分　　好吧，隨便妳。　喬

B **1.** What is NOT true about the TV programs tonight?
   A. There's more than one movie.
   B. There's a program about birds.
   C. One of the programs is about music.
   D. The TV guide lists programs on two channels.

關於今晚的電視節目，哪一項不正確？
A. 不只有一部電影。
B. 有個關於鳥類的節目。
C. 其中一個節目是關於音樂。
D. 電視節目表列出了兩個頻道的節目。

理由

問題類型： 細節題

根據電視節目表，沒有任何節目是關於鳥類，故 B 項敘述錯誤，應為正選。

CH
2

C **2.** What do we know about Daisy and Joe?
   A. They don't live together.
   B. Daisy likes travel stories.
   C. Daisy doesn't like frightening movies.
   D. Joe is going to stay at his friend's house tonight.

關於黛西和喬，我們得知哪一項？
A. 他們沒有同住。
B. 黛西喜歡旅行故事。
C. 黛西不喜歡恐怖片。
D. 喬今晚要待在朋友家。

理由

問題類型： 推論題

根據訊息第五條第一句 "I don't want to be frightened and have bad dreams!"（我不想被嚇到做惡夢！），得知 C 項應為正選。

B **3.** Which TV program did Daisy and Joe agree on?
   A. *Fly Away Today*
   B. *Sooner or Later*
   C. *Music Is My Life*
   D. *One of Us Must Know*

黛西和喬講好要看哪一個電視節目？
A.《萬里翱遊》
B.《緣來擋不住》
C.《音樂人生》
D.《搞鬼你或我》

理由

問題類型： 細節題

訊息第四條第三句喬提議看十點的電影，根據節目表得知為 *One of Us Must Know*《搞鬼你或我》，但黛西接著表示不想看恐怖片，堅持要看他們講好的愛情故事，由節目表可知為 *Sooner or Later*《緣來擋不住》，故 B 項應為正選。

🏷️ 重要單字片語

1. **channel** [ˈtʃænļ] *n.* 頻道（後面常與介詞 on 並用）；管道；海峽

2. **travel** [ˈtrævļ] *n.* 旅行（指「長途旅行」時為複數，指「旅行的行為」時為不可數）& *vi.* 旅行

3. **sooner or later**　遲早

4. **couple** [ˈkʌpļ] *n.* 夫婦或情侶；一對，一雙，幾個
   a couple of...　幾個……；一對……

5. **scared** [skɛrd] *a.* 害怕的
   be scared of...
= be afraid of...

6. **keep sb up**　使某人睡不著

7. **discuss** [dɪˈskʌs] *vt.* 討論

8. **probably** [ˈprɑbəbļɪ] *adv.* 很可能

9. **make it (to...)**　及時趕到（某處）

10. **frightened** [ˈfraɪtņd] *a.* 受到驚嚇的
    be frightened of...　害怕……
= be afraid of...
    frightening [ˈfraɪtņɪŋ] *a.* 令人害怕的

11. **whatever** [(h)watˈɛvɚ] *pron.* 任何東西

From:	adam.richards@richards-motors.com
To:	all.staff@richards-motors.com
Subject:	Company Barbecue

Hi,

I would like to invite you all to a barbecue at my house this Saturday starting at 2 p.m. It is my way of saying thank you for your hard work during these past few months. It has been one of our busiest periods, and I'm proud of how well we've handled it. No one needs to bring any food or drink. My wife will prepare a salad, my son will make pizza, my daughter will make dessert, and I'll cook the meat. I hope to see everyone there!

Adam

CH
2

Elaine Hey, Jan. Are you feeling OK after this afternoon's barbecue?   10:05 p.m.

10:06 p.m.   Not really. I've got stomachache. **Jan**

Elaine Me, too! I think it was the cream cake. I thought the cream smelled bad at the time.   10:06 p.m.

10:07 p.m.   I knew I shouldn't have eaten it, but I was being polite. **Jan**

Elaine At least the weather was nice and sunny. I had good fun in the pool.   10:08 p.m.

10:08 p.m.   Yeah, that was great. There wasn't much to drink, though. How can he only offer Coke and water? **Jan**

Elaine Beats me! I'll take my own next time!   10:09 p.m.

寄件者：	adam.richards@richards-motors.com
收件者：	all.staff@richards-motors.com
主 旨：	公司烤肉聚會

大家好：

我想邀請各位在這個星期六到我家來參加下午兩點開始的烤肉聚會。我要用這個方式來感謝你們在過去這幾個月的努力工作。這段時間是我們最忙碌的時期之一，我很驕傲大家都處理得非常好。不需要帶任何食物或飲料。我太太要拌沙拉，我兒子做披薩，女兒做甜點，我來烤肉。大家都要來喔！

亞當

伊蓮 嘿，珍。下午烤肉會完後妳感覺 OK 嗎？　晚上十點五分

　　　　　晚上十點六分　　不 OK。我肚子痛。　**珍**

伊蓮 我也是耶！我猜是那個鮮奶油蛋糕。我那時就覺得鮮奶油聞起來怪怪的。　晚上十點六分

　　　　　晚上十點七分　　我就知道我不該吃，但又不想失禮。　**珍**

伊蓮 至少今天天氣很好。我在游泳池裡玩得很開心。　晚上十點八分

　　　　　晚上十點八分　　是啊，游泳池不錯。不過飲料太少了。他怎麼會只有可樂和開水呢？　**珍**

伊蓮 天知道！下次我自己帶飲料！　晚上十點九分

A 1. What do we learn about Richards Motors?
A. It is doing well.
B. It is closing early.
C. It is losing money.
D. It is hiring new workers.

關於理查茲汽車公司，我們得知什麼？
A. 它生意不錯。
B. 它要提早打烊。
C. 它在賠錢。
D. 它在招募新員工。

理由

問題類型： 推論題

根據電子郵件內文第三句 "It has been one of our busiest periods, and I'm proud of how well we've handled it."（這段時間是我們最忙碌的時期之一，我很驕傲大家都處理得非常好。），可推知該公司員工因為公司前陣子生意不錯而工作忙碌，故 A 項應為正選。

D 2. What else do Elaine and Jan complain about besides the cake?
A. The pool
B. The people
C. The weather
D. The drink selection

伊蓮和珍除了蛋糕之外還抱怨什麼？
A. 游泳池
B. 人
C. 天氣
D. 飲料種類

理由

問題類型： 細節題

她們於聊天室第一至三段抱怨鮮奶油蛋糕似乎壞掉導致她們肚子痛，最後兩段又抱怨現場提供的飲料選擇不多，故 D 項應為正選。

D 3. Who prepared the food that Elaine and Jan think made them ill?
A. Adam
B. Adam's son
C. Adam's wife
D. Adam's daughter

誰準備的食物讓伊蓮和珍身體不舒服？
A. 亞當
B. 亞當的兒子
C. 亞當的太太
D. 亞當的女兒

理由

問題類型： 多文本整合題

根據電子郵件內文倒數第二句 "My wife will prepare a salad, my son will make pizza, my daughter will make dessert, and I'll cook the meat."（我太太要拌沙拉，我兒子做披薩，女兒做甜點，我來烤肉。）及聊天室第三段第二、三句伊蓮說 "I think it was the cream cake. I thought the cream smelled bad at the time."（我猜是那個鮮奶油蛋糕。我那時就覺得鮮奶油聞起來怪怪的。），得知是亞當女兒做的甜點蛋糕造成客人身體不舒服，故 D 項應為正選。

📑 重要單字片語

1. **barbecue** [ˈbɑrbɪkju] *n.* 烤肉聚會（可縮寫為 BBQ）

2. **period** [ˈpɪrɪəd] *n.* 時期；時代

3. **be proud of...** 以……為榮

4. **handle** [ˈhændḷ] *vt.* 處理，應付

5. **smell + adj.** 聞起來……

6. **polite** [pəˈlaɪt] *a.* 禮貌的；有禮貌的

7. **(it) beats me** 你問倒我了，我也搞不清楚

8. **selection** [səˈlɛkʃən] *n.* 可供挑選的東西

A Note to Our Guests

We hope you are enjoying your stay at the Happy Healthy Hotel. Some of our services will need to close briefly for repair work. Please see the table below for further information.

Happy Healthy Hotel—Repair Work	
Date	Area Affected
July 14th	Inside pool
July 15th	Gym
July 16th	Outside pool
July 17th	Bar & restaurant

To apologize for any trouble, we are offering guests 50% off a two-night stay in our sister hotel, the Feeling Fine Hotel, which looks over the river.

From:	jim.hsieh@coldmail.com
To:	pam.lien@coldmail.com
Subject:	Thanks

Dear Pam,

Thank you so much for giving me a birthday I will never forget. I wasn't expecting that at all! The meal in the hotel restaurant was excellent. I don't think I've ever eaten such perfectly cooked fish! It was nice to sit by the pool, too, although I was sad that the outside pool was closed. I'm looking forward to our stay in the Feeling Fine Hotel. Thanks again.

Jim

給貴賓們的通知

希望您在悅康飯店住得滿意。有幾項服務因進行維修工程將暫停提供。詳情請見下表。

悅康飯店 —— 維修工程	
日期	受影響區域
七月十四日	室內游泳池
七月十五日	健身房
七月十六日	室外游泳池
七月十七日	酒吧與餐廳

我們對於造成各位困擾表達歉意，因此將提供各位貴賓在我們的姊妹飯店 —— 俯瞰河景的安康飯店 —— 入住兩晚的半價折扣。

寄件者：	jim.hsieh@coldmail.com
收件者：	pam.lien@coldmail.com
主 旨：	謝謝妳

親愛的潘：

非常感謝妳給了我一個難以忘懷的生日。我都沒有預料到耶！飯店餐廳的餐點真好吃。我想我從來沒吃過烹調得那麼完美的魚！坐在游泳池邊的感覺也很好，雖然室外游泳池沒開放我很難過。我很期待要去住安康飯店。再次感謝妳。

吉姆

C 1. How is the Happy Healthy Hotel saying sorry to its guests?

A. By taking them on a boat trip along the river

B. By offering them a free meal at the restaurant

C. By offering them a cheaper stay at another hotel

D. By taking money off their bill at the Happy Healthy Hotel

悅康飯店如何對貴賓表達歉意？

A. 帶他們搭船遊河

B. 提供他們在餐廳免費吃一頓

C. 提供他們在另一間飯店住宿的優惠價

D. 他們在悅康飯店的住宿可享折扣

理由

問題類型：細節題

根據公告最後兩行 "To apologize for any trouble, we are offering guests 50% off a two-night stay in our sister hotel, the Feeling Fine Hotel, which looks over the river."（我們對於造成各位困擾表達歉意，因此將提供各位貴賓在我們的姊妹飯店 —— 俯瞰河景的安康飯店 —— 入住兩晚的半價折扣。），得知 C 項應為正選。

B 2. What do we learn about Jim and Pam?

A. Jim is a better swimmer than Pam.

B. Pam surprised Jim with the hotel stay.

C. Pam and Jim are brother and sister.

D. Jim and Pam prefer the Feeling Fine Hotel.

關於吉姆和潘，我們得知哪一項？

A. 吉姆游泳比潘游得好。

B. 潘帶吉姆去飯店住宿，讓他很意外。

C. 潘和吉姆是兄妹。

D. 吉姆和潘比較喜歡安康飯店。

理由

問題類型：推論題／多文本整合題

吉姆在電子郵件內文前兩句感謝潘給了他一個難忘的生日，讓他感到很意外，而第五句提及室外游泳池不開放，與悅康飯店維修公告裡泳池維修的資訊相符，可推知他們是去悅康飯店住宿，故 B 項應為正選。

C 3. When did Jim and Pam visit the Happy Healthy Hotel?

A. On July 14th

B. On July 15th

C. On July 16th

D. On July 17th

吉姆和潘是在何時光顧悅康飯店？

A. 七月十四日

B. 七月十五日

C. 七月十六日

D. 七月十七日

理由

問題類型：多文本整合題

電子郵件內文第三句提及 "The meal in the hotel restaurant was excellent."（飯店餐廳的餐點真好吃。），根據悅康飯店的維修公告，七月十七日餐廳未營業；第五句提及 "It was nice to sit by the pool, too, although I was sad that the outside pool was closed."（坐在游泳池邊的感覺也很好，雖然室外游泳池不開放我很難過。），根據維修公告，室外游泳池受維修工程影響的時間是七月十六日，七月十四、十五日室外游泳池未受影響，故 **C** 項應為正選。

🏷️ 重要單字片語

1. **briefly** [`briflɪ] *adv.* 短暫地；簡短地

2. **affect** [ə`fɛkt] *vt.* 影響；（疾病）侵襲

3. **bar** [bɑr] *n.* 酒吧，吧臺；棒；條

4. **expect** [ɪk`spɛkt] *vt.* 預料；期待，等待

5. **excellent** [`ɛkslənt] *a.* 很棒的；傑出的

6. **perfectly** [`pɝfɪktlɪ] *adv.* 完美地；完全地

7. **prefer** [prɪ`fɝ] *vt.* 較喜歡

   prefer A to B　　喜歡 A 甚於 B

   prefer to V rather than V　　喜歡做……甚於做……

= prefer to V instead of + V-ing

Seaton High School welcomes parents and families to our...

Sports Day!

All of our students have been training hard for their events and are looking forward to showing off to their moms and dads. Please see below for the list of events.

Seaton High School Sports Day	
Time	**Event**
1:00 p.m.	100-meter race
1:30 p.m.	500-meter race
2:00 p.m.	Long jump
2:30 p.m.	High jump

Free drinks and snacks are available in the school lunch room.

These have been kindly provided by a local company.

From:	ninarobertson123@coldmail.com
To:	principal@seaton-high-school.com
Subject:	Sports Day

Mr. Skinner,

I am writing this email to say thank you for a successful and well-organized sports day. My husband and I took the afternoon off work to watch our daughter Lisa take part in—and win!—the 100-meter race. We stayed for the whole afternoon and really enjoyed it. All of the other parents, family members, and students seemed to be having a great time, too. And the juice and the lemon cake were delicious!

Thanks again.

Nina

希頓高中歡迎家長及子女蒞臨我們的……

運動會！

我們所有的學生都在為他們各自的比賽而努力訓練，期待要在爸爸媽媽面前表現一下。

請參閱下方的比賽時程表。

希頓高中運動會	
時間	比賽
下午一點	一百公尺賽跑
下午一點三十分	五百公尺賽跑
下午兩點	跳遠
下午兩點三十分	跳高

學校餐廳裡有免費飲料和點心。

由一家本地公司熱心提供。

寄件者：	ninarobertson123@coldmail.com
收件者：	principal@seaton-high-school.com
主　旨：	運動會

史基納先生：

我寫這封電子郵件是為了感謝您舉辦了一場成功而籌劃完備的運動會。我和我先生下午請假去看我們的女兒麗莎參加一百公尺賽跑，而且她贏了！我們待了整個下午，看得非常開心。

其他家長、家人和學生似乎也都很開心。而且果汁和檸檬蛋糕都很可口！

再次感謝。

妮娜

B **1.** What do we know about the food at the sports day?
   A. The food was quite expensive.
   B. The food was provided by a local business.
   C. The students made the food by themselves.
   D. The food was sold at stands around the playground.

關於運動會提供的食物，我們得知什麼？
A. 食物相當貴。
B. 食物是由一家當地企業提供的。
C. 食物是學生親手做的。
D. 食物在操場四周的攤位販賣。

理由

問題類型：細節題

根據運動會傳單的最下方兩句 "Free drinks and snacks are available in the school lunch room. These have been kindly provided by a local company."（學校餐廳裡有免費飲料和點心。由一家本地公司熱心提供。），得知 B 項應為正選。

D **2.** What is true about Nina?
   A. She attended the sports day alone.
   B. She didn't try the free juice or cake.
   C. She left right after her daughter's event.
   D. She used personal leave to attend the sports day.

關於妮娜，哪一項是正確的？
A. 她一個人去了運動會。
B. 她沒有品嚐免費果汁或蛋糕。
C. 她在女兒的比賽結束後就馬上離開。
D. 她用個人休假去看運動會。

理由

問題類型：細節題

根據電子郵件內文第二句 "My husband and I took the afternoon off work to watch our daughter Lisa take part in—and win!—the 100-meter race."（我和我先生下午請假去看我們的女兒麗莎參加一百公尺賽跑，而且她贏了！），得知 D 項應為正選。

A **3.** What time was Nina's daughter's event?
   A. At 1:00 p.m.
   B. At 1:30 p.m.
   C. At 2:00 p.m.
   D. At 2:30 p.m.

妮娜女兒的比賽是幾點？
A. 下午一點
B. 下午一點半
C. 下午兩點
D. 下午兩點半

理由

問題類型：多文本整合題

根據電子郵件內文第二句 "My husband and I took the afternoon off work to watch our daughter Lisa take part in—and win!—the 100-meter race."（我和我先生下午請假去看我們的女兒麗莎參加一百公尺賽跑，而且她贏了！）及運動會傳單內比賽時程表第三列 100-meter race（一百公尺賽跑）的時間為 1:00 p.m.（下午一點），得知 A 項應為正選。

CH 2

🏷 重要單字片語

1. **train** [tren] *vi.* & *vt.*（為參加某比賽而）訓練，操練（常與介詞 for 並用）

2. **event** [ɪ`vɛnt] *n.*（比賽）項目；活動；事件

3. **show off**　　表現自己，炫耀，賣弄
   show off sth / show sth off　　炫耀某物

4. **(the) long jump**　　跳遠

5. **(the) high jump**　　跳高

6. **snack** [snæk] *n.* 點心，零食

7. **successful** [sək`sɛsfəl] *a.* 成功的

8. **well-organized** [`wɛl`ɔrɡə,naɪzd] *a.* 組織良好的

9. **take + 一段時間 + off (work / school)**
   （跟公司／學校）請（一段時間）的假
   take a day off　　請一天的假
   take the afternoon off　　請下午的假

10. **member** [`mɛmbɚ] *n.* 成員

11. **stand** [stænd] *n.* 攤位 & *vi.* 站立 & *vt.* 忍受

12. **playground** [`ple,ɡraʊnd] *n.*（學校）操場；遊樂場

13. **leave** [liv] *n.* 假；假期 & *vi.* & *vt.* 離開

THE GREAT GAMES STORE

New Games Available on September 27th	
The Lost Darkness	An exciting game set in a future when the sun never goes down
Faster, Faster, Faster 5: Don't Stop	The latest racing game on the most popular tracks
To The Death	Fight insects from space in this fun new fighting game
Super Sports Fun	Try your hand at a range of different sports in this new game

Please note that on the first day, we will only have 100 copies of each game in store. More will be available in the following days.

CH
2

NEW GAME REVIEW

By Max Mitchell

Games Reporter

My son has been looking forward to getting a new video game for his game machine, and he loves fighting games. I, on the other hand, have been excited for months about the new racing game. I've played and completed the earlier four games, and I hoped that the new one would not let me down. And it didn't! The **graphics** are excellent. Everything on the screen looks very real. It's also nice to race around different tracks and in different places. I am now looking forward to the next one!

超讚遊戲專賣店

九月二十七日開賣的新款遊戲	
《消失的暗黑》	這款刺激遊戲的場景設定在未來一個太陽永不西沉的世界
《疾速賽車 5：永不停歇》	最新賽車遊戲，模擬幾個最受歡迎的跑道
《蟲蟲殊死大戰》	來試試這個好玩的新款戰鬥遊戲，和太空昆蟲搏鬥吧
《超能運動員》	來玩玩這款新遊戲裡一系列不同的運動，試試身手

請注意：開賣第一天，店裡每款遊戲將只提供一百份。

接下來幾天會有更多貨。

新款電玩評論

作者：電玩記者 麥克斯・米契爾

我兒一直很期待為他的電玩主機添購新遊戲，他很喜歡戰鬥遊戲。我則是為新一代賽車遊戲興奮了好幾個月。我已經玩過並完勝前四代遊戲，希望這次的新遊戲不會讓我失望。結果真的沒有！裡面的畫質超強。螢幕上所有東西看起來都很逼真。在不同賽道和不同地點競速也很過癮。我現在已經在期待下一代的遊戲了！

__D__ **1.** What is true about The Great Games Store?
A. It sells over one hundred different games.
B. It mainly sells fighting and sports games.
C. It won't sell the new games until October.
D. It only has a limited number of the new games.

關於超讚遊戲專賣店，哪一項敘述正確？
A. 該店販賣超過一百種不同的遊戲。
B. 該店主要販賣戰鬥類及運動類遊戲。
C. 該店十月才會販賣新款遊戲。
D. 該店僅有限量的新款遊戲。

理由

問題類型：細節題
根據廣告內容倒數第二行 "Please note that on the first day, we will only have 100 copies of each game in store."（請注意：開賣第一天，店裡每款遊戲將只提供一百份。），得知 D 項應為正選。

__B__ **2.** What does "**graphics**" in Max's review probably mean?
A. People who make a computer game
B. Pictures shown on a computer screen
C. The tracks based on a computer racing game
D. Images shown on a computer game box

麥克斯評論裡的 graphics 一字可能是什麼意思？
A. 製作電腦遊戲的人
B. 電腦螢幕上顯示的圖畫
C. 電腦賽車遊戲中的跑道
D. 電腦遊戲盒上的圖樣

理由

問題類型：推論題
根據後一句 "Everything on the screen looks very real."（螢幕上所有東西看起來都很逼真。），可推知 graphics 指遊戲的畫面，故 B 項應為正選。

__B__ **3.** Which game did Max review?
A. *The Lost Darkness*
B. *Faster, Faster, Faster 5: Don't Stop*
C. *To The Death*
D. *Super Sports Fun*

麥克斯的評論是針對哪一款遊戲？
A.《消失的暗黑》
B.《疾速賽車 5：永不停歇》
C.《蟲蟲殊死大戰》
D.《超能運動員》

理由

問題類型：多文本整合題
評論第二句 "I, on the other hand, have been excited for months about the new racing game."（我則是為新一代賽車遊戲興奮了好幾個月。）、第三句 "I've played and completed the earlier four games, ..."（我已經玩過且完勝前四代遊戲……）及倒數第二句 "It's also nice to race around different tracks and in different places."（在不同賽道和不同地點競速也很過癮。）均與廣告中的賽車遊戲 *Faster, Faster, Faster 5: Don't Stop*（《疾速賽車 5：永不停歇》）描述相符，得知 B 項應為正選。

重要單字片語

1. **darkness** [ˈdɑrknɪs] *n.* 黑暗
2. **race** [res] *vi.* 疾馳；疾走
   racing [ˈresɪŋ] *n.* （競速）比賽
3. **insect** [ˈɪnsɛkt] *n.* 昆蟲
4. **try one's hand**　某人試手氣，某人嘗試
5. **range** [rendʒ] *n.* 系列商品；範圍
   a range of...　一系列……

6. **on the other hand**　另一方面（前面常與 on the one hand（一方面）並用）
7. **complete** [kəmˈplit] *vt.* 完成（本文中指遊戲破關）& *a.* 完全的；完整的
8. **let sb down**　讓某人失望
9. **graphics** [ˈgræfɪks] *n.* （電腦）繪圖（恆為複數）
10. **limited** [ˈlɪmɪtɪd] *a.* 有限的

West City Hospital

Visitors Policy

Rule 1	Visits are allowed from 2 p.m. to 4 p.m. and 6 p.m. to 8 p.m. on weekdays, and 8 a.m. to 8 p.m. on weekends.
Rule 2	All visitors must report to the main desk in the department they wish to visit and get a visitor's pass.
Rule 3	Please wash your hands before going in to see the patient.
Rule 4	Please do not sit on the patient's bed.

Please note: Hospital parking is limited.
Visitors are advised to use other means.

CH
2

Fred I went to see Chris in the hospital this morning.   8:30 p.m.

8:31 p.m.   How is he? I haven't gone to see him yet. I've got stomachache. **Jenna**

Fred He is recovering from the operation quite well. Something strange happened, though. One of the nurses asked me to leave!   8:31 p.m.

8:33 p.m.   Did you go there outside of visiting hours? **Jenna**

Fred No. She said I shouldn't sit on Chris's bed because of hospital rules. She was quite serious.   8:34 p.m.

8:35 p.m.   I guess they've got these rules to keep the patients safe and healthy. **Jenna**

Fred You should remember that when you go visit him!   8:36 p.m.

西城醫院

訪客規定

規定一	平日開放探視時間為下午兩點至四點及下午六點至八點，週末為早上八點至晚上八點。
規定二	所有訪客需至欲探視的科別之主服務臺報到及領取訪客通行證。
規定三	請洗完手後再入內探視病人。
規定四	請勿坐在病床上。

請注意：醫院停車位有限。

建議訪客使用其他交通工具。

弗瑞德　我今天早上去醫院看克里斯了。　晚上八點三十分

晚上八點三十一分　他還好嗎？我還沒去看他。我胃不舒服。　**珍娜**

弗瑞德　他動完手術後復原得很好。不過發生了一件奇怪的事。有一位護理師竟然要我離開！　晚上八點三十一分

晚上八點三十三分　你是在非探視時間去那裡的嗎？　**珍娜**

弗瑞德　不是。她說我不該坐在克里斯的病床上，因為醫院有規定。她非常認真。　晚上八點三十四分

晚上八點三十五分　我想他們訂這些規定是為了維護病人的安全和健康。　**珍娜**

弗瑞德　所以妳去看他時要記得這規定喔！　晚上八點三十六分

A 1. What are visitors to West City Hospital advised NOT to do?
   A. Drive to the hospital
   B. Bring a gift for the patient
   C. Visit on weekday evenings
   D. Stay for longer than one hour

建議去西城醫院的訪客不要做什麼？
A. 開車去醫院
B. 送禮給病人
C. 週間晚上探視
D. 探視超過一小時

理由

問題類型： 細節題

根據醫院訪客規定後的備註 "Hospital parking is limited. Visitors are advised to use other means."（醫院停車位有限。建議訪客使用其他交通工具。），得知院方建議訪客不要開車去，故 A 項應為正選。

A 2. What do we know from Fred's and Jenna's messages?
   A. Chris's health is improving.
   B. Jenna is going to the hospital the next day.
   C. Fred visited the patient during the wrong hours.
   D. Chris is staying at the hospital because of a stomachache.

從弗瑞德與珍娜的對話訊息中可以得知什麼？
A. 克里斯的健康狀況正在好轉。
B. 珍娜隔天要去醫院。
C. 弗瑞德在錯誤時段去探視病人。
D. 克里斯因為胃痛正在住院中。

理由

問題類型： 細節題

根據聊天室訊息第三段第一句弗瑞德回覆 "He is recovering from the operation quite well."（他動完手術後復原得很好。），得知 A 項應為正選。

D 3. Which hospital rule did Fred break?
   A. Rule 1
   B. Rule 2
   C. Rule 3
   D. Rule 4

弗瑞德違反了哪一項醫院規定？
A. 規定一
B. 規定二
C. 規定三
D. 規定四

理由

問題類型： 多文本整合題

根據聊天室訊息第五段第二句弗瑞德回覆 "She said I shouldn't sit on Chris's bed because of hospital rules."（她說我不該坐在克里斯的病床上，因為醫院有規定。）及醫院訪客規定四 "Please do not sit on the patient's bed."（請勿坐在病床上。），得知 D 項應為正選。

📑 重要單字片語

1. **policy** [ˈpɑləsɪ] *n.* 規定；政策
2. **report** [rɪˈpɔrt] *vi.* 報到 & *vt.* 報導 & *n.* 報告
3. **patient** [ˈpeʃənt] *n.* 病人 & *a.* 有耐心的
4. **means** [minz] *n.* 手段，方法，工具（單複數同形）
5. **stomachache** [ˈstʌməkˌek] *n.* 胃痛，肚子痛
6. **recover** [rɪˈkʌvɚ] *vi.* 恢復健康
   recover from... 從……復原
7. **operation** [ˌɑpəˈreʃən] *n.* 手術（可數）；（機器）運轉（不可數）
8. **serious** [ˈsɪrɪəs] *a.* 嚴肅的，認真的；嚴重的
9. **improve** [ɪmˈpruv] *vi.* 改善 & *vt.* 改良

Hi, Ben,

I'll be home late tonight. A woman from the office is leaving today, so we're all going out for a meal with her after work. Your dad will be late, too, as he needs to work late. Please use one of the food ordering apps on the iPad to order yourself some dinner. Don't spend over $10, and try to order something with some vegetables! Remember to do your homework, and don't have any wild parties!

Love, Mom

FFF: Fast Fresh Food Straight to Your Home!		
Menu		
Item	**Information**	**Price**
Beef Sandwich	Toasted sandwich with beef and cheese	$10
Pizza Surprise	Pizza with lots of vegetables	$7.50
Chicken Noodles	Hot noodles with chicken	$9.50
Super Vegetables	A black rice dish with cream and vegetables	$12.50

Please note:

· An extra charge of $2 will be added to each order.

· We promise the food will arrive within 40 minutes.

· If we fail to deliver your food within 40 minutes, you will get 25% off your next order.

嗨，班：

我今天會晚回家。辦公室有位女同事今天要離職，所以下班後我們所有人要和她出去吃飯。你爸爸也會晚回家，因為他要加班。你用 *iPad* 裡的點餐應用程式叫晚餐來吃。不要花超過十美元，而且盡量點有蔬菜的！記得寫功課，還有不要亂開趴！

愛你的 老媽

三福外送：快速鮮食直送府上！
菜單

項目	內容	價格
牛肉三明治	夾牛肉與起司的烤三明治	10 美元
驚喜披薩	有大量蔬菜的披薩	7.50 美元
雞湯麵	熱的雞肉湯麵	9.50 美元
超級蔬食總匯	有奶油與蔬菜的紫米飯	12.50 美元

請注意：

· 每份訂單將加收兩美元。

· 我們保證餐點在四十分鐘內送達。

· 如果我們未能在四十分鐘內送達，您下次的訂單將打七五折。

D 1. Why will Ben's mom be late home?

    A. She is leaving her job today.

    B. She is going out with Ben's dad.

    C. She has to work late in the office.

    D. She is going out with friends from work.

班的媽媽為什麼會晚回家？

A. 她今天要離職。

B. 她要和班的爸爸出門。

C. 她得在辦公室加班。

D. 她要和同事出去。

理由

問題類型： 細節題

根據留言內文第二句 "A woman from the office is leaving today, so we're all going out for a meal with her after work."（辦公室有位女同事今天要離職，所以下班後我們所有人要和她出去吃飯。），得知 D 項應為正選。

C 2. Ben's food took one hour to arrive. What will Ben get?
A. A special free dessert
B. A message saying sorry
C. Money off his next order
D. His money back for the order

班的餐點一小時才送達。班會得到什麼？
A. 一份特別的免費甜點
B. 一則表達歉意的訊息
C. 下次訂單的折扣
D. 退還訂餐的錢

理由

問題類型：**情境題**

根據菜單附註第二、三點 "We promise the food will arrive within 40 minutes. If we fail to deliver your food within 40 minutes, you will get 25% off your next order."（我們保證餐點在四十分鐘內送達。如果我們未能在四十分鐘內送達，您下次的訂單將打七五折。），得知 C 項應為正選。

B 3. According to Ben's mother's advice, what should Ben order?
A. Beef Sandwich
B. Pizza Surprise
C. Chicken Noodles
D. Super Vegetables

根據班的媽媽的建議，班應該點哪一項餐點？
A. 牛肉三明治
B. 驚喜披薩
C. 雞湯麵
D. 超級蔬食總匯

理由

問題類型：**多文本整合題**

班的媽媽在留言內文倒數第二句交代班點餐時要注意 "Don't spend over $10, and try to order something with some vegetables!"（不要花超過十美元，而且盡量點有蔬菜的！），根據菜單第二項餐點，Pizza Surprise（驚喜披薩）為 Pizza with lots of vegetables（有大量蔬菜的披薩），且價格為 7.50 美元，低於十美元，故 B 項應為正選。

🏷️ 重要單字片語

1. **app** [æp] *n.* 應用程式（為 application [ˌæpləˋkeʃən] 的縮寫）

2. **wild** [waɪld] *a.* 瘋狂的；狂野的；野生的

3. **toast** [tost] *vt.* 烤，烘；向……敬酒 & *n.* 吐司（不可數）
（本文中 toasted 為過去分詞作形容詞用）

4. **extra** [ˋɛkstrə] *a.* 額外的 & *n.* 額外（收費）的事物

5. **promise** [ˋprɑmɪs] *vt.* 承諾 & *n.* 諾言
promise to V　承諾要做……
promise sb sth　承諾某人某事……
promise sb (that)...　承諾某人……

6. **advice** [ədˋvaɪs] *n.* 建議，忠告（不可數）
a piece of advice　一個建議
= a suggestion
some advice　一些建議
= some suggestions

REPORT CARD

Name of Student: Emma Aceveda

Subject	Grade	Comments
English	A	Emma continues to be an excellent student, getting top grades for all of her papers. It's clear she loves reading.
History	D	Emma did really well in this class last year, but this year the quality of her work has started to go down.
Art	D	Emma tries her best, but it seems she is not a natural artist.
Math	B	Emma has dealt well with the difficult work this year. She can work out the answers quickly in her head.

Dear Mrs. Aceveda,

Your daughter Emma is always very polite and friendly. She comes to class on time and always hands in her homework on time. She seemed to be really interested in the topics we studied last year and always got high grades. However, this year, she is getting poor grades. I am not sure if she is not interested in what we're studying, or if there are problems at home or with her friends. Please let me know when you are free to come to the school to discuss this with me.

Thank you.

Mr. Vendrell

成績單		
學生姓名：艾瑪 · 艾希維達		
科目	**成績**	**評語**
英文	A	艾瑪表現依然優秀，她所有的報告都拿到最高分。顯然她很喜歡閱讀。
歷史	D	艾瑪去年在這門課的表現優異，不過她的課業品質今年卻開始下滑了。
美術	D	艾瑪盡力了，但她似乎不是天生的畫家。
數學	B	艾瑪今年對難題處理得不錯。她可以迅速在腦中盤算出如何作答。

CH
2

艾希維達太太您好：

令嬡艾瑪向來非常有禮貌又和氣。她準時上課，也總是按時交作業。她似乎對我們去年的學習主題很感興趣，而且總能得到高分。然而今年她的成績很不好。我不確定她是否對目前的學習內容沒興趣，還是有家庭或朋友相處的問題。請告知您何時方便來學校與我討論此事。

謝謝您。

凡德雷爾老師

B **1.** What do we know from Emma's school report?

A. Emma is interested in art.

B. Emma gets top grades in English.

C. Emma struggles to do math in her head.

D. Emma got different grades in all the four subjects.

從艾瑪的成績單可以得知什麼？

A. 艾瑪對美術感興趣。

B. 艾瑪在英文科拿到最高分。

C. 艾瑪在腦中解數學題很掙扎。

D. 艾瑪這四科得到的分數都不一樣。

理由

問題類型：　細節題

根據成績單第四列 English（英文）第三欄 Comments（評語）的第一句 "Emma continues to be an excellent student, getting top grades for all of her papers."（艾瑪表現依然優秀，她所有的報告都拿到最高分。），得知 B 項應為正選。

D **2.** What does Mr. Vendrell NOT suggest might be Emma's problem?
   A. She might have lost interest in the subject.
   B. She might have difficulties with her friends.
   C. She might be having trouble with her parents.
   D. She might be finding the lessons too difficult.

凡德雷爾老師對於艾瑪的問題，沒有提到哪一項？
   A. 她可能對該科目失去興趣。
   B. 她可能跟朋友相處有困難。
   C. 她可能跟父母間有親子問題。
   D. 她可能覺得課程太難。

理由

問題類型：　細節題

根據凡德雷爾老師來信內文倒數第二句 "I am not sure if she is not interested in what we're studying, or if there are problems at home or with her friends."（我不確定她是否對目前的學習內容沒興趣，還是有家庭或朋友相處的問題。），並未提及艾瑪也許覺得課程太難，故 D 項應為正選。

B **3.** Which subject does Mr. Vendrell teach?
   A. English
   B. History
   C. Art
   D. Math

凡德雷爾老師教哪一科？
   A. 英文
   B. 歷史
   C. 美術
   D. 數學

理由

問題類型：　多文本整合題

根據成績單第五列 History（歷史）第三欄 Comments（評語）"Emma did really well in this class last year, but this year the quality of her work has started to go down."（艾瑪去年在這門課的表現優異，不過她的課業品質今年卻開始下滑了。）及凡德雷爾老師的來信內文第三、四句 "She seemed to be really interested in the topics we studied last year and always got high grades. However, this year, she is getting poor grades."（她似乎對我們去年的學習主題很感興趣，而且總能得到高分。然而今年她的成績很不好。），得知 B 項應為正選。

重要單字片語

1. **a report card**　成績單
2. **grade** [gred] *n.* 成績，分數；年級 & *vt.*
    打成績
3. **quality** [ˋkwɑlətɪ] *n.* 品質
4. **go down**　下降，降低
5. **deal with...**　處理 / 應付……
6. **work out sth / work sth out**
    想出……；計算出……

7. **on time**　準時
    in time　及時
8. **hand in...**　呈交 / 繳交……
    = **turn in...**
9. **topic** [ˋtɑpɪk] *n.* 主題；議題
10. **do math in sb's head**
    在腦中計算數學題

Study Desk 405

You should have received the following items:

· 1 large desk top

· 1 desk back

· 4 desk legs

· 1 raised computer screen table

· 8 large nails

· 4 small nails

Please follow these steps:

1. Lay the desk top on the floor and use 4 large nails to fix the desk legs.

2. Use the other 4 large nails to fix the desk back.

3. Turn over your desk and stand it on the ground.

4. Use the 4 small nails to fix the raised computer screen table.

Please note that Study Chair 405 must be bought separately.

From:	keith.cotton@zmail.com
To:	customer-service@desksareus.com
Subject:	Study Desk 405—Order Number DSD4051287

Dear Customer Service,

I recently ordered the above item from your online store. It arrived quickly and was packed well. When I fixed the legs to the top of the desk, it was clear that the quality of the wood was very good. However, when I began to fix the desk back to the main part of the desk, I realized that the other four large nails were missing. Could you please send these out to me as soon as possible?

Thank you.

Keith Cotton

405 型書桌

您應該收到了下列物件：

- 一張大型桌面
- 一片桌背
- 四支桌腳
- 一組電腦螢幕墊高架
- 八根大型釘子
- 四根小型釘子

請按下列步驟組裝：

1. 將桌面平放地面，用四根大型釘子安裝桌腳。

2. 用另外四根大型釘子安裝桌背。

3. 將桌子翻轉站立於地面。

4. 用四根小型釘子安裝電腦螢幕墊高架。

請注意：405 型書椅須另購。

寄件者：	keith.cotton@zmail.com
收件者：	customer-service@desksareus.com
主　旨：	405 型書桌 —— 訂單編號 DSD4051287

客服人員你好：

我最近在你們的網路商店訂購了上面這項商品。商品很快就送來了，而且包裝得很好。當我把桌腳安裝到書桌桌面時，很明顯看出木材的質料蠻不錯的。不過當我準備把桌背安裝到書桌主體時，才發現短少了另外四根大型釘子。可否盡快把它們寄給我？

謝謝。

凱斯・卡登

C **1.** What is true about Study Desk 405?
A. It comes in different colors.
B. It is supplied with an office chair.
C. It comes with a small raised table.
D. It is supplied with a set of drawers.

關於 405 型書桌，哪一項敘述正確？
A. 它有不同顏色可供選擇。
B. 它配有一張辦公椅。
C. 它附有一組小型墊高架。
D. 它配有一組抽屜。

理由

問題類型： 細節題
根據說明書中的配備物件第四項 1 raised computer screen table（一組電腦螢幕墊高架），
得知 C 項應為正選。

A **2.** Which part of Study Desk 405 does Keith NOT say positive things about?
A. The cost of the items
B. The speed of the order
C. The safety of the packing
D. The quality of the material

關於 405 型書桌的優點，凱斯沒有提
到哪一部分？
A. 商品的價格
B. 訂單處理的速度
C. 包裝的安全性
D. 製材的品質

理由

問題類型： 細節題
電子郵件內文第二句 "It arrived quickly and was packed well."（商品很快就送來了，而且
包裝得很好。）提及 B、C 項，第三句 "... the quality of the wood was very good."（……
木材的質料蠻不錯的。）提及 D 項，全文並未提及 A 項，故應為正選。

B **3.** Which step of the guide was Keith unable to complete?
A. Step 1
B. Step 2
C. Step 3
D. Step 4

凱斯無法完成組裝指南的哪一個步驟？
A. 步驟一
B. 步驟二
C. 步驟三
D. 步驟四

理由

問題類型： 多文本整合題
電子郵件內文第四句提及 "However, when I began to fix the desk back to the main part
of the desk, I realized that the other four large nails were missing."（不過當我準備把
桌背安裝到書桌主體時，才發現短少了另外四根大型釘子。），而根據說明書中的配備物件第
五項 8 large nails（八根大型釘子）及組裝步驟二 "Use the other 4 large nails to fix the
desk back."（用另外四根大型釘子安裝桌背。），得知步驟二缺少另外四根大型釘子無法完
成，故 B 項應為正選。

重要單字片語

1. **desk top**　　桌面
   desk back　　桌背

2. **raise** [rez] *vt.* 提高；舉起；撫養，飼養；募集
   （本文中 raised 為過去分詞作形容詞用，表「墊高的」）

3. **screen** [skrin] *n.* 螢幕；屏幕

4. **turn over... / turn... over**　　翻轉……

5. **stand** [stænd] *vt. & vi.*（使）直立 / 站立；豎放

6. **separately** [ˋsɛpərɪtlɪ] *adv.* 單獨地，各自地

7. **quality** [ˋkwɑlətɪ] *n.* 品質；特質

8. **supply** [səˋplaɪ] *vt.* 提供，供應 & *n.* 補給品（恆用複數）；供給量
   supply A with B　　提供 B 給 A

9. **a set of...**　　一組……

10. **drawer** [ˋdrɔɚ] *n.* 抽屜

11. **positive** [ˋpɑzətɪv] *a.* 正面的；積極的；確定的

12. **speed** [spid] *n.* 速度

13. **material** [məˋtɪrɪəl] *n.* 材料，原料（可數）；資料，題材（不可數）

14. **guide** [gaɪd] *n.* 指南；指引；嚮導 & *vt.* 指導
    a guide dog　　導盲犬
    = **a seeing-eye dog**

15. **be unable to V**　　無法做……

16. **complete** [kəmˋplit] *vt.* 完成 & *a.* 完全的；完整的；完成的

	Job Interviews for Assistant Manager	
	Monday, October 18th	
Time	**Name**	**Comments**
09:00	Tasha Rodriguez	Has a master's degree in business studies, but no real-world experience
09:30	Neil Imperioli	Used to be a manager for a huge clothes company, but now wants a lower-stress job
10:00	Pia Delaney	Is currently an assistant manager at another computer firm like ours, but is looking to move somewhere new
10:30	Vernon Falco	Has worked in this company for years and is looking to earn more money

From:	ssullivan@placer-computers.com
To:	ecooper@placer-computers.com
Subject:	Today's Interviews

Hi Emily,

Sorry to email you so early, but I wanted to let you know that I will miss one of the interviews today. I have an important meeting with the director of sales at 10:30, so I will need to give the last interview a miss. However, I'm sure that you are more than able to do the interview on your own. I hope your visit to the dentist went well, by the way. Let's go out for lunch when I've finished my meeting.

Sylvie

CH
2

應徵副理面試表

十月十八日星期一

時間	姓名	備註
九點	塔莎·羅德里格斯	有商業研究碩士學位，但沒有實務經驗
九點三十分	尼爾·英普雷歐李	曾是一家大型服飾公司的經理，但現在想找一份壓力較小的工作
十點	琵雅·德萊尼	目前是另一家像我們這樣的電腦公司的副理，但打算換個工作環境
十點三十分	弗農·法爾可	已在本公司任職多年，想多賺點錢

寄件者：	ssullivan@placer-computers.com
收件者：	ecooper@placer-computers.com
主　旨：	今天的面試

嗨，艾蜜莉：

很抱歉這麼早發電子郵件給妳，我只是想告訴妳今天的其中一場面試我不會參與。我十點半和業務部主管有個重要會議，所以我不得不缺席最後一場面試。不過我確信妳絕對有能力獨自主持面試。順帶一提，希望妳看牙醫一切順利。我開完會後咱們一起去吃午飯吧。

席薇

C 1. What is correct about the people who have applied for the job?

A. Pia Delaney does not work in the industry.

B. Neil Imperioli would like to be a manager.

C. Tasha Rodriguez has never had a job before.

D. Vernon Falco works for a clothes company.

關於應徵這份工作的人，哪一項是正確的？

A. 琵雅‧德萊尼不在這個行業上班。

B. 尼爾‧英普雷歐李想當經理。

C. 塔莎‧羅德里格斯從未工作過。

D. 弗農‧法爾可在服飾公司工作。

理由

問題類型： 細節題

根據應徵副理面試表第四列第三欄關於 Tasha Rodriguez（塔莎‧羅德里格斯）的 Comments（備註）：Has a master's degree in business studies, but no real-world experience（有商業研究碩士學位，但沒有實務經驗），得知 C 項應為正選。

D 2. What do we know about Emily?

A. She will cancel her visit to the dentist.

B. She will meet the director in place of Sylvie.

C. She won't be able to have lunch with Sylvie.

D. She receives Sylvie's email on the interview day.

關於艾蜜莉，我們得知什麼？

A. 她將取消看牙醫的行程。

B. 她將代替席薇會見主管。

C. 她將無法跟席薇共進午餐。

D. 她在面試日收到席薇的電子郵件。

理由

問題類型： 細節題

根據電子郵件的 Subject（主旨）：Today's Interviews（今天的面試）及內文第一句 "Sorry to email you so early, but I wanted to let you know that I will miss one of the interviews today."（很抱歉這麼早發電子郵件給妳，我只是想告訴妳今天的其中一場面試我不會參與。），得知 D 項應為正選。

D 3. Whose interview will Sylvie miss?

A. Tasha Rodriguez's

B. Neil Imperioli's

C. Pia Delaney's

D. Vernon Falco's

席薇會錯過誰的面試？

A. 塔莎‧羅德里格斯的

B. 尼爾‧英普雷歐李的

C. 琵雅‧德萊尼的

D. 弗農‧法爾可的

理由

問題類型： 多文本整合題

根據電子郵件第二句 "I have an important meeting with the director of sales at 10:30, so I will need to give the last interview a miss."（我十點半和業務部主管有個重要會議，所以我不得不缺席最後一場面試。）及應徵副理面試表最後一列 10:30（十點三十分）的應徵者為 Vernon Falco（弗農‧法爾可），得知 D 項應為正選。

🏷 重要單字片語

1. **assistant** [ə'sɪstənt] *a.* 助理的 & *n.* 助理

2. **a master's degree**　碩士學位
   a bachelor's degree　學士學位

3. **used to V**　過去曾做……
   be used to + N/V-ing　習慣於……

4. **currently** ['kɝəntlɪ] *adv.* 目前

5. **look to V**　打算／想要做……

6. **director** [də'rɛktɚ] *n.* 主管；主任；導演

7. **dentist** ['dɛntɪst] *n.* 牙醫
   the dentist　牙醫診所
   = **the dentist's**

8. **industry** ['ɪndəstrɪ] *n.* 行業（可數）；工業（不可數）

9. **cancel** ['kænsḷ] *vt.* 取消

10. **in place of...**　代替／取代……

SuperShop Department Store		
Floor Guide		
Floor	**Store Information**	**Other Information**
1F	Rings & watches, glasses & sunglasses, pictures & gifts, ladies' & men's shoes, children's shoes, bags & purses	Ladies' restroom, information desk
2F	Ladies' formal clothes, ladies' informal clothes, men's formal clothes, men's informal clothes, sports goods, summer clothes	Ladies' & men's restrooms
3F	Children's clothes, children's toys, kitchen items, bedding & towels	Family restroom
4F	Western & Asian restaurants, wine shop, movie theater	Ladies' & men's restrooms

Gabriel Have you finished yet? I want to go up to the fourth floor and get something to eat. 3:42 p.m.

3:44 p.m. Not yet. I'm looking for new T-shirts for Matthew. He's already grown out of those ones we got him for Christmas. Then, I want to get a new cover for his bed. **Olivia**

Gabriel We've been in here for hours! 3:45 p.m.

3:48 p.m. Why don't you go downstairs and look for some new golf clubs? **Olivia**

Gabriel I don't need any. 3:49 p.m.

3:53 p.m. OK, I'll try to be quick. **Olivia**

Gabriel Thank you. I get to pick the restaurant! 3:53 p.m.

超級購百貨公司		
樓層導覽		
樓層	**商店資訊**	**其他資訊**
一樓	戒指和手錶、眼鏡和太陽眼鏡、掛畫和禮品、女鞋和男鞋、童鞋、包袋和女用小包	女廁、服務臺
二樓	正式女裝、休閒女裝、正式男裝、休閒男裝、運動用品、夏季服裝	女廁和男廁
三樓	童裝、兒童玩具、廚房用品、寢具和毛巾	親子廁所
四樓	西式與亞洲料理餐廳、紅酒專賣店、電影院	女廁和男廁

**CH
2**

加百利亞 妳好了嗎？我想上去四樓吃東西。　下午三點四十二分

下午三點四十四分　還沒。我在幫馬修找新 T 恤。我們聖誕節時幫他買的那幾件他現在已經穿不下了。然後我想幫他買新的床罩。　**奧莉薇亞**

加百利亞 我們已經在這裡待好幾個小時了！　下午三點四十五分

下午三點四十八分　你去樓下看看新的高爾夫球桿好了。　**奧莉薇亞**

加百利亞 我不需要。　下午三點四十九分

下午三點五十三分　好吧，我盡量快一點。　**奧莉薇亞**

加百利亞 謝謝。餐廳歸我選！　下午三點五十三分

C **1.** Which of the following items could you buy on the first floor?

A. A nice bottle of red wine

B. A new towel for the beach

C. A watch for a special birthday

D. A man's suit for an important event

在一樓可以買到下列哪一項物品？

A. 一瓶不錯的紅酒

B. 一條新的海灘浴巾

C. 為特別重要的生日準備的手錶

D. 某重要活動時穿的男士西裝

理由

問題類型：細節題

根據樓層導覽一樓的資訊，該樓層有販售 Rings & watches（戒指和手錶），得知 C 項應為正選。

B **2.** What do we know about Olivia and Gabriel?

A. They both need new T-shirts.

B. They have a son named Matthew.

C. They prefer western to Asian food.

D. They are shopping for Christmas presents.

關於奧莉薇亞與加百利亞，我們知道哪一項？

A. 他們倆人都需要新的 T 恤。

B. 他們有個兒子名叫馬修。

C. 他們喜歡西式食物勝過亞洲食物。

D. 他們在選購聖誕禮物。

理由

問題類型：推論題

根據聊天室對話第二段第二至四句，奧莉薇亞說 "I'm looking for new T-shirts for Matthew. He's already grown out of those ones we got him for Christmas. Then, I want to get a new cover for his bed."（我在幫馬修找新 T 恤。我們聖誕節時幫他買的那幾件他現在已經穿不下了。然後我想幫他買新的床罩。），可推知馬修是奧莉薇亞與加百利亞的兒子，故 B 項應為正選。

C **3.** Which floor of the department store are Olivia and Gabriel currently on?

A. The first floor

B. The second floor

C. The third floor

D. The fourth floor

奧莉薇亞與加百利亞正在百貨公司的哪一個樓層？

A. 一樓

B. 二樓

C. 三樓

D. 四樓

理由

問題類型：多文本整合題

根據聊天室對話第二段第二至四句，奧莉薇亞正在選購童裝和寢具，另根據樓層導覽三樓的商店資訊，該樓層有販售 Children's clothes（童裝）及 bedding & towels（寢具和毛巾），得知他們正在三樓，故 C 項應為正選。

重要單字片語

1. **ring** [rɪŋ] *n.* 戒指；鈴聲；環狀物 & *vi.* (鈴聲) 響起

2. **purse** [pɝs] *n.* 女用小型手提包 (= handbag)

3. **restroom** [ˋrɛst͵rum] *n.* (公共) 洗手間，廁所

4. **the information desk** 服務臺

5. **formal** [ˋfɔrml̩] *a.* 正式的

6. **informal** [ɪnˋfɔrml̩] *a.* 非正式的

7. **bedding** [ˋbɛdɪŋ] *n.* 寢具；被褥

8. **towel** [ˋtauəl] *n.* 毛巾

9. **grow out of...** (小孩) 長大而穿不下 (原來的衣服)

10. **cover** [ˋkʌvɚ] *n.* 罩子；蓋子；封面 & *vt.* 覆蓋；掩飾；涵蓋

11. **go downstairs** 下樓
    go upstairs 上樓

12. **a golf club** 高爾夫球桿

13. **suit** [sut] *n.* 套裝；西裝

14. **prefer A to B** 喜歡 A 甚於 B

CH 2

https://www.student-paper.com — ☐ ✕

STUDENT ELECTION ENDS IN SURPRISE

The student government election ended in surprise late last night as Diana Garcia was elected head of the government. Miss Garcia received 41% of the vote. The person in second place—third-year student Miguel Rivera—received 33%. It was widely believed that Mr. Rivera, the most popular one in the election, would win. Many students admitted to not knowing who Miss Garcia was. However, she gained a lot of support on social media in the days leading up to the election. The other two students—Albert Nguyen and Elora Torres—each got 13% of the vote.

Dear Diary,

I woke up this morning and saw the election results online. "Surprise" didn't come close to describing how I felt. I had never even heard of Diana Garcia until last week, and now she's going to be the head of the student government! She got over 40% of the vote, while my guy only got a third. I hope Diana Garcia has got some good policies rather than just an ability to make eye-catching posts on social media. Only time will tell, I guess.

Helen

https://www.student-paper.com

學生會選舉結果爆冷門

學生會選舉的結果昨天深夜出爐後大爆冷門，戴安娜・賈西亞被選為學生會會長。賈西亞同學獲得 41% 選票。名列第二的三年級生米格爾・里維拉獲得 33% 選票。人們普遍認為選舉大熱門的里維拉同學會獲勝。許多學生承認不知道賈西亞是何方神聖。然而在選舉之前的幾天內，她在社群媒體獲得不少支持。另外兩位同學 —— 亞伯特・阮和艾羅拉・托瑞斯 —— 各獲得 13% 選票。

親愛的日記：

我今早醒來在網路上看到選舉結果。「驚訝」一字實不足以形容我的感受。直到上週我才聽說戴安娜・賈西亞這個人，而現在她就要當上學生會會長了！她獲得超過 40% 選票，而我支持的人只拿到三分之一。我希望戴安娜・賈西亞拿出好政策，而不是只有在社群媒體上發布吸睛貼文這種能力。我想只有時間才能證明一切吧。

海倫

D **1.** How did Diana Garcia probably win the election?
  A. By delivering a funny speech
  B. By coming up with great policies
  C. By giving free cakes to the students
  D. By becoming popular on social media

戴安娜・賈西亞很可能靠什麼贏得選舉？
  A. 藉由發表一場搞笑的演講
  B. 藉由提出好政策
  C. 藉由發送免費蛋糕給學生
  D. 藉由在社群媒體上炒人氣

理由

問題類型：推論題

根據網路新聞內文倒數第二句 "However, she gained a lot of support on social media in the days leading up to the election."（然而，在選舉之前的幾天內，她在社群媒體獲得不少支持。），可推知賈西亞在選舉前利用社群媒體提升人氣可能是勝選的關鍵，故 D 項應為正選。

C **2.** Why did Helen write in her diary?
　　A. To express her joy
　　B. To say she is sorry
　　C. To express her doubts
　　D. To say she was wrong

海倫為何要寫這篇日記？
A. 表達她的喜悅
B. 説她很抱歉
C. 表示她的懷疑
D. 説她錯了

理由

問題類型：<u>主旨題</u>

根據日記內文倒數兩句 "I hope Diana Garcia has got some good policies rather than just an ability to make eye-catching posts on social media. Only time will tell, I guess."（我希望戴安娜・賈西亞拿出好政策，而不是只有在社群媒體上發布吸睛貼文這種能力。我想只有時間才能證明一切吧。），可推知海倫對賈西亞同學的領導能力感到懷疑，故 C 項應為正選。

C **3.** Who did Helen vote for in the student government election?
　　A. Elora Torres
　　B. Diana Garcia
　　C. Miguel Rivera
　　D. Albert Nguyen

海倫在學生會的選舉中投票給誰？
A. 艾羅拉・托瑞斯
B. 戴安娜・賈西亞
C. 米格爾・里維拉
D. 亞伯特・阮

理由

問題類型：<u>多文本整合題</u>

根據日記倒數第三句 "She got over 40% of the vote, while my guy only got a third."（她獲得超過 40% 選票，而我支持的人只拿到三分之一。）及網路新聞內文第三句 "The person in second place—third-year student Miguel Rivera—received 33%."（名列第二的三年級生米格爾・里維拉獲得 33% 選票。），得知海倫支持的人是 Miguel Rivera，故 C 項應為正選。

🏷 重要單字片語

1. **election** [ɪˈlɛkʃən] *n.* 選舉
2. **government** [ˈɡʌvɚnmənt] *n.* 政府；政體
　　the student government　　學生會
3. **receive** [rɪˈsiv] *vt.* 收到；接到

4. **vote** [vot] *n.* 選票總數（前面加 the）；投票 & *vi.* 投票
5. **admit** [ədˈmɪt] *vi.* & *vt.* 承認（三態為：admit, admitted [ədˈmɪtɪd], admitted）
　　admit to + N/V-ing　　承認……

6. **support** [sə`pɔrt] *n.* & *vt.* 支持

7. **media** [`midɪə] *n.* 媒體（複數形，單數
形為 medium [`midɪəm]）
social media　　社群媒體

8. **lead up to...**　　發生在……之前

9. **sb wake up**　　某人醒來
比較: wake sb up　　叫醒某人

10. **result** [rɪ`zʌlt] *n.* 結果

11. **hear of...**　　聽說過……
比較: hear from...　　收到……的消息

12. **eye-catching** [`aɪ,kætʃɪŋ] *a.* 引人注目
的

13. **(Only) time will tell.**　　（只有）時間
會證明一切。

14. **deliver** [dɪ`lɪvɚ] *vt.* 發表（演講）；遞送

15. **come up with...**　　提出／想出……

16. **express** [ɪk`sprɛs] *vt.* 表達

CH
2

https://www.nightbikerides.com — □ ✕

The Best Night Rides in Hope Town

Bicycle rides at night are popular during the summer because of the cooler evening temperatures. Let's look at four of the best in Hope Town.

Ride A This takes you up into the hills to get a great view of the city.

Ride B This easy ride takes you along the town's beautiful river.

Ride C This ride takes you through the city's busy streets—why not stop for a drink or snack along the way?

Ride D This difficult ride takes you on a trip through the woods.

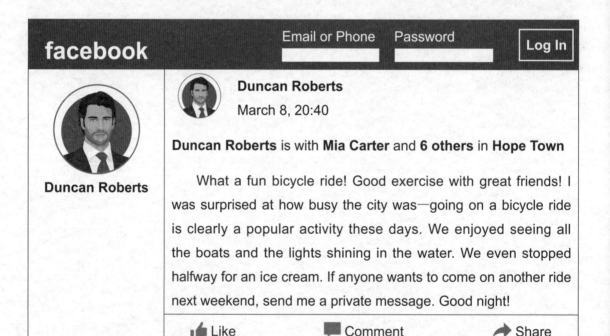

facebook   Email or Phone   Password   Log In

Duncan Roberts

Duncan Roberts
March 8, 20:40

Duncan Roberts is with **Mia Carter** and **6 others** in **Hope Town**

What a fun bicycle ride! Good exercise with great friends! I was surprised at how busy the city was—going on a bicycle ride is clearly a popular activity these days. We enjoyed seeing all the boats and the lights shining in the water. We even stopped halfway for an ice cream. If anyone wants to come on another ride next weekend, send me a private message. Good night!

👍 Like   💬 Comment   ➤ Share

https:// www.nightbikerides.com   — ▢ ✕

希望城最佳夜騎行程

夏日的傍晚氣溫較涼爽,因此夜騎廣受歡迎。

一起來看看希望城的四條最佳行程。

A 路線 這條路線帶你上山一覽本市的美景。

B 路線 這條低難度路線帶你沿著城區的美麗河道暢行。

C 路線 這條路線帶你穿過本市熱鬧的街道 —— 半路上可停下腳步喝杯飲料或吃個點心。

D 路線 這條高難度路線帶你穿過森林。

---

facebook   電子郵件或電話   密碼   登入

鄧肯 · 羅伯茲

鄧肯 · 羅伯茲

三月八日晚上八點四十分

鄧肯 · 羅伯茲和米亞 · 卡特以及**其他六個人**在**希望城**

這次的單車之旅真好玩!好運動有好友相伴!城區的熱鬧讓我很驚訝 —— 騎單車顯然是最近很受歡迎的活動。我們飽覽水上船隻以及映照在水面閃爍的燈光。甚至在半路上停下來吃冰淇淋。如果有人下個週末想再騎一趟,可以私訊我。晚安!

👍 讚   💬 留言   ➤ 分享

B **1.** What does nightbikerides.com say about summer night rides?

A. They are easier than day rides.

B. The weather isn't as hot at night.

C. They don't require bicycle lights.

D. The summer months are less popular.

關於夏天夜騎，單車夜騎網說了什麼？

A. 夜騎比白天騎車來的容易。

B. 夜間天氣不會那麼熱。

C. 夜騎不需要開腳踏車燈。

D. 夏季月份中比較少人夜騎。

理由

問題類型：細節題

根據網頁內容第二至三行 "Bicycle rides at night are popular during the summer because of the cooler evening temperatures."（夏日的傍晚氣溫較涼爽，因此夜騎廣受歡迎。），得知 B 項應為正選。

A **2.** What does Duncan NOT say in his Facebook post?

A. Bicycle rides are a good way to make friends.

B. There may be another ride next week.

C. There were more people than he expected.

D. They enjoyed a sweet treat during the ride.

鄧肯在他的臉書貼文中沒有提到哪一項？

A. 騎單車是交到朋友的好方法。

B. 下禮拜可能會再騎一次。

C. 人比他預期的多。

D. 他們在騎車途中享用了甜食。

理由

問題類型：細節題

臉書貼文段落倒數第二句 "If anyone wants to come on another ride next weekend, send me a private message."（如果有人下個週末想再騎一趟，可以私訊我。）暗示之後可能會再騎一次，即 B 項敘述；而第三及第五句分別提及 C、D 項；另貼文中僅提到與好朋友一起去騎，並未提及藉由活動本身可交到新朋友；故 A 項應為正選。

C **3.** Which ride did Duncan and his friends go on?

A. Ride A

B. Ride B

C. Ride C

D. Ride D

鄧肯和他的朋友走了哪一條路線？

A. A 路線

B. B 路線

C. C 路線

D. D 路線

理由

問題類型： 多文本整合題

根據臉書貼文段落第四、五句 "We enjoyed seeing all the boats and the lights shining in the water. We even stopped halfway for an ice cream."（我們飽覽水上船隻以及映照在水面閃爍的燈光。甚至在半路上停下來吃冰淇淋。）及網頁內容 C 路線的敘述 "This ride takes you through the city's busy streets—why not stop for a drink or snack along the way?"（這條路線帶你穿過本市熱鬧的街道 —— 半路上可停下腳步喝杯飲料或吃個點心。），得知 C 項應為正選。

重要單字片語

1. **temperature** [ˋtɛmp(ə)rətʃɚ] *n.* 溫度；體溫

2. **woods** [wʊdz] *n.* 樹林；森林（常用複數）

3. **password** [ˋpæsˌwɚd] *n.* 密碼

4. **log in**　　登入／進入（電腦系統）

5. **shine** [ʃaɪn] *vi.* 照耀，發亮 & *vt.* 擦亮

    注意
    shine 的三態有兩種：
    照耀 (*vi.*)：shine, shone [ʃon], shone
    擦亮 (*vt.*)：shine, shined, shined

6. **halfway** [ˋhæfˋwe] *adv.* 中途；半路上

7. **private** [ˋpraɪvɪt] *a.* 私人的；私立的
    in private　　私底下

8. **treat** [trit] *n.* 美食；樂事；款待，請客 & *vt.* 招待；對待；治療

TOY WONDER WORLD

GRAND SALE!

To celebrate the opening of our new store, we are having a grand sale!

See below for our best deals!

Item	Was	Now
Animal Puzzle—put together this picture showing the animals of the world	$19.99	$9.99
Be A Soccer Star—everything you need to be a great player	$29.99	$14.99
Dino the Dog—this cute little toy dog acts just like a real pet!	$39.99	$19.99
Total Turtles—one of today's most popular video games	$49.99	$24.99

Dear Grandma Alice and Grandpa Pete,

I am writing this note to say thank you very much for my birthday present. I love it! Mom and Dad won't let me have a pet because they say I don't know how to look after one. So, this is the next best thing! I will take him everywhere I go, just like a real dog. This way, I can show them that they can trust me to look after a real dog, too!

Lots of love,

Timmy

玩具奇妙世界

大拍賣！

為了慶祝新店面開幕，我們將舉辦特賣會！

請參閱以下最划算的商品價格！

商品	原價	優惠價
動物拼圖 —— 拼好圖畫就可以看到世界上的動物	19.99 美元	9.99 美元
來當足球明星 —— 當一名偉大球員所需要的一切東西	29.99 美元	14.99 美元
狗狗迪諾 —— 這隻可愛的玩具小狗動作就像真的寵物！	39.99 美元	19.99 美元
烏龜總動員 —— 目前最受歡迎的電玩之一	49.99 美元	24.99 美元

親愛的愛麗絲奶奶和彼特爺爺：

我寫這張便條是想感謝你們送我生日禮物。我很喜歡它！爸爸媽媽不會讓我養寵物，因為他們說我不懂怎麼照顧寵物。所以這是僅次於寵物最好的東西了！我去任何地方都會帶著它，就像照顧真的狗一樣。這樣我就能跟爸媽證明，他們可以信任我也能照顧一隻真的狗！

致上滿滿的愛，

提米

<u>D</u> **1.** What is true about the sale at Toy Wonder World?

    A. It only lasts for one week.

    B. It only includes animal toys.

    C. It is because a store is closing.

    D. Its best deals are all half price.

關於玩具奇妙世界的特賣會，哪一項是正確的？

    A. 只持續一星期。

    B. 只賣動物玩具。

    C. 因為有一家店要結束營業而舉辦。

    D. 所有優惠價皆為半價。

理由

問題類型：<u>細節題</u>

根據商品優惠價目表推算得知表中四項商品的優惠價均為原價的一半左右，故 D 項應為正選。

<u>C</u> **2.** Why does Timmy talk about his parents in the note?

    A. They want to say thank you.

    B. They want to return the gift.

    C. They won't let him have a pet.

    D. They made him write the note.

提米為何在便條中談到他父母？

    A. 他們想道謝。

    B. 他們想退還禮物。

    C. 他們不會讓他養寵物。

    D. 他們要他寫這張便條。

理由

問題類型：<u>細節題</u>

根據便條內文第三句 "Mom and Dad won't let me have a pet because they say I don't know how to look after one."（爸爸媽媽不會讓我養寵物，因為他們說我不懂怎麼照顧寵物。），得知 C 項應為正選。

<u>C</u> **3.** How much did Grandma Alice and Grandpa Pete spend on Timmy's gift?

    A. $9.99

    B. $14.99

    C. $19.99

    D. $24.99

愛麗絲奶奶和彼特爺爺花了多少錢買送給提米的禮物？

    A. 9.99 美元

    B. 14.99 美元

    C. 19.99 美元

    D. 24.99 美元

理由

問題類型：<u>推論題 / 多文本整合題</u>

根據便條內文第三至四句 "Mom and Dad won't let me have a pet because... So, this is the next best thing!"（爸爸媽媽不會讓我養寵物，因為……。所以這是僅次於寵物最好的東西了！），可推知爺爺奶奶送提米的禮物是玩具小狗，而商品優惠價目表第三項商品 "**Dino the Dog**—this cute little toy dog acts just like a real pet!"（**狗狗迪諾** —— 這隻可愛的玩具小狗動作就像真的寵物！）的優惠價為 19.99 美元，故 C 項應為正選。

重要單字片語

1. **grand** [grænd] *a.* 盛大的；重大的；豪華的

2. **celebrate** [ˈsɛləˌbret] *vt.* 慶祝

3. **deal** [dil] *n.* 交易，買賣；協議
   a good deal　（買東西）價格便宜

4. **item** [ˈaɪtəm] *n.* 物品，品項

5. **put together sth / put sth together**
   拼合／組裝某物

6. **act** [ækt] *vi.* 舉止；行為 & *n.* 作為

7. **total** [ˈtotḷ] *a.* 完全的，徹底的

8. **turtle** [ˈtɝtḷ] *n.* 烏龜

9. **look after...**　照顧……

10. **the next best thing**
    僅次於最好的／退而求其次的事物

11. **trust** [trʌst] *vt.* & *n.* 信任

CH 2

Welcome to
Music Conversations!

We're the online room for all music lovers.
Please follow the rules of the room, as listed below.

Rule 1: Do not use the room to run your own business or sell your own products.
Rule 2: Do not send any message that includes bad language.
Rule 3: Do not ask for the full name or address of any other member of the group.
Rule 4: Do not attack anyone personally for their opinions.

Anyone found to be breaking these rules will be asked to leave the room and will not be allowed back for a period of one month.

Debra Hey! Has anyone in here listened to the new Bruno Mars album? 8:30 p.m.

8:31 p.m. Of course! He's my favorite singer. **Chris**

Debra Cool. He's mine, too! What do you love about him? 8:31 p.m.

8:35 p.m. I like the way his music mixes many different styles like rock and soul. What about you? **Chris**

Debra I love the words in his songs. They mean a lot to me. 8:36 p.m.

8:36 p.m. Maybe we could meet up and listen to him together. What's your last name, Debra? Where do you live? **Chris**

Debra I don't think that's such a good idea. Maybe we should stop talking. 8:38 p.m.

歡迎來到
音樂對談！

我們是開放給所有愛樂者的線上聊天室。

請遵守聊天室公約，詳列於下方。

公約一：勿利用聊天室經營自己的事業或販售自己的商品。

公約二：勿傳送任何包含不雅文字的訊息。

公約三：勿詢問群組裡其他成員的全名或住址。

公約四：勿因任何人的言論對其作人身攻擊。

發現違反上述公約情事者，將被要求離開聊天室且一個月內不得返回。

黛博拉　嗨！有人聽了火星人布魯諾的新專輯嗎？　晚上八點三十分

晚上八點三十一分　當然有！他是我最喜歡的歌手。　**克里斯**

黛博拉　酷。他也是我的最愛！你喜歡他哪一點？　晚上八點三十一分

晚上八點三十五分　我喜歡他的音樂結合許多不同的風格，像是搖滾樂和靈魂樂。妳呢？　**克里斯**

黛博拉　我喜歡他歌曲裡的歌詞。對我來說它們意義非凡。　晚上八點三十六分

晚上八點三十六分　或許我們可以見個面，一起聽他的歌。黛博拉，妳姓什麼？住哪裡？　**克里斯**

黛博拉　我不覺得這是個好主意。也許我們不該再聊了。　晚上八點三十八分

B **1.** What happens if you break a rule of the online room?
A. You can't come back at any point.
B. You can't come back for a few weeks.
C. You have to pay a fine to the manager.
D. You have to say sorry to other members.

如果違反線上聊天室公約會發生什麼事？
A. 永遠不得回到群組裡。
B. 幾週內不得回到群組裡。
C. 得付罰款給管理員。
D. 得向其他成員道歉。

理由

問題類型： 細節題

根據聊天室公告倒數兩行 "Anyone found to be breaking these rules will be asked to leave the room and will not be allowed back for a period of one month."（發現違反上述公約情事者，將被要求離開聊天室且一個月內不得返回。），得知 B 項應為正選。

C **2.** What does Debra like about the singer's songs?
A. The way the music is written
B. The way different styles are mixed
C. The way the words are written
D. The way the songs make her dance

黛博拉喜歡那位歌手歌曲的哪個方面？
A. 作曲的方式
B. 結合不同風格的方式
C. 作詞的方式
D. 歌曲讓她想隨之起舞的方式

理由

問題類型： 細節題

根據對話第五段 "I love the words in his songs. They mean a lot to me."（我喜歡他歌曲裡的歌詞。對我來說它們意義非凡。），得知 C 項應為正選。

C **3.** Which rule did Chris break?
A. Rule 1
B. Rule 2
C. Rule 3
D. Rule 4

克里斯違反了哪一條公約？
A. 公約一
B. 公約二
C. 公約三
D. 公約四

理由

問題類型： 多文本整合題

根據對話倒數第二段第二、三句，克里斯問黛博拉 "What's your last name, Debra? Where do you live?"（黛博拉，妳姓什麼？住哪裡？）及聊天室公告中的公約三 "Do not ask for the full name or address of any other member of the group."（勿詢問群組裡其他成員的全名或住址。），得知 C 項應為正選。

📑 重要單字片語

1. **run** [rʌn] *vt.* 經營 & *vi.* 奔跑;(機器)運作(三態為:run, ran [ræn], run)

2. **product** [ˋprɑdʌkt] *n.* 產品;產物

3. **attack** [əˋtæk] *vt.* & *n.* 攻擊

4. **personally** [ˋpɝsṇlɪ] *adv.* 針對個人;親自

5. **opinion** [əˋpɪnjən] *n.* 意見
   in one's opinion　依某人之見
   = in one's view

6. **album** [ˋælbəm] *n.*(音樂)專輯;相簿
   release an album　發行專輯

7. **style** [staɪl] *n.* 風格;形式

8. **rock** [rɑk] *n.* 搖滾樂(不可數);岩石(可數)& *vt.* & *vi.* 搖動(= shake)

9. **soul** [sol] *n.* 爵士靈歌;靈魂;人(可數)

10. **meet up**　碰面;相聚

11. **last name**　姓
    first name　名

12. **fine** [faɪn] *n.* 罰金(可數)& *a.* 安好的 & *vt.*(對……)罰款

CH
2

Real Town Airport – Flights Leaving		
Time	To	Flight No.
16:40	Tokyo	IT 6834
17:10	Manila	PA 9821
17:40	Seoul	IT 1348
18:10	Kuala Lumpur	KL 4492

Passengers are advised to check the weight limits with their airline. Any bag that is over the weight limit will be charged extra. Also, no sharp objects are allowed in any carry-on bags. Please arrive at the airport three hours before the flight takes off.

Adam Where are you? We're going to be late for the flight! 14:39

14:40 I'm sorry! I got held up at work. I'm nearly home now. **Irene**

Adam Who cares about work at a time like this? Our flight leaves in three hours! 14:40

14:42 We've got lots of time. Even with traffic, we'll be at the airport by 15:40. **Irene**

Adam But I don't want to rush. 14:43

14:44 Don't worry. I think I'll still have lots of time to have my pre-flight drink and look around in the shops. ☺ **Irene**

瑞爾鎮機場 —— 班機起飛告示		
時間	目的地	班機編號
下午四點四十分	東京	IT 6834
下午五點十分	馬尼拉	PA 9821
下午五點四十分	首爾	IT 1348
下午六點十分	吉隆坡	KL 4492

旅客請事先向航空公司查詢行李重量限制。超重行李將加收費用。同時，登機行李內不得有尖銳物品。請在班機起飛前三小時到達機場。

CH 2

亞當 妳在哪裡？我們快要趕不上班機了！　　下午兩點三十九分

下午兩點四十分　　對不起！工作忙耽擱了。我快到家了。　　**艾琳**

亞當 在這種時候誰還會在乎工作啊？我們的班機三　　下午兩點四十分
小時後就要起飛了！

下午兩點四十二分　　時間還很充裕。就算塞車，我們也可以在　　**艾琳**
三點四十分前到機場。

亞當 但我不想弄得那麼趕。　　下午兩點四十三分

下午兩點四十四分　　別擔心。我想我還會有不少時間可以在登機　　**艾琳**
前喝一杯，然後逛逛商店。☺

D 1. Which of the following is NOT advised by Real Town Airport?

A. Passengers should arrive at the airport early.

B. Passengers should not carry dangerous items.

C. Passengers should check how heavy their bags are.

D. Passengers should leave their cars in the parking lot.

瑞爾鎮機場沒有建議下列哪一件事？

A. 乘客應提早抵達機場。

B. 乘客不應攜帶危險物品。

C. 乘客應確認他們的行李重量。

D. 乘客應將車停在停車場。

理由

問題類型：細節題

班機起飛告示下方說明第一句 "Passengers are advised to check the weight limits with their airline."（旅客請事先向航空公司查詢行李重量限制。）、第三句 "Also, no sharp objects are allowed in any carry-on bags."（同時，登機行李內不得有尖銳物品。）及第四句 "Please arrive at the airport three hours before the flight takes off."（請在班機起飛前三小時到達機場。）分別提及 C、B、A 項，唯未對停車部分做任何建議，故 D 項應為正選。

A 2. Why is Adam worried about getting to the airport on time?

A. He doesn't want to have to hurry.

B. He needs to do work at the airport.

C. He hopes to go shopping at the airport.

D. He wants to have a coffee at the airport.

亞當為什麼擔心無法準時趕到機場？

A. 他不想搞得匆匆忙忙。

B. 他必須到機場處理公事。

C. 他希望能在機場逛街購物。

D. 他想在機場喝杯咖啡。

理由

問題類型：細節題

根據聊天室對話倒數第二段亞當的留言 "But I don't want to rush."（但我不想弄得那麼趕。），得知 A 項應為正選。

C 3. Where are Adam and Irene flying to?

A. Tokyo

B. Manila

C. Seoul

D. Kuala Lumpur

亞當和艾琳要搭飛機去哪裡？

A. 東京

B. 馬尼拉

C. 首爾

D. 吉隆坡

理由

問題類型：多文本整合題

根據聊天室對話第三段亞當於下午兩點四十分的留言第二句 "Our flight leaves in three hours!"（我們的班機三小時後就要起飛了！），得知他們的班機起飛時間為下午五點四十分，對照班機起飛告示第五列後得知於此時間起飛的班機目的地為 Seoul（首爾），故 C 項應為正選。

🏷️ 重要單字片語

1. **airport** [ˈɛrˌpɔrt] *n.* 機場
2. **flight** [flaɪt] *n.* 班機，航班；飛行
3. **weight** [wet] *n.* 重量；體重
4. **limit** [ˈlɪmɪt] *n.* 上限，限制 & *vt.* 限制
5. **airline** [ˈɛrˌlaɪn] *n.* 航空公司
6. **object** [ˈɑbdʒɪkt] *n.* 東西，物體
7. **carry-on** [ˈkærɪˌɑn] *a.* 可隨身攜帶登機的 & *n.* 隨身行李

8. **take off** （飛機等）起飛
9. **get / be held up** 被耽擱 / 延誤
10. **rush** [rʌʃ] *vi.* & *vt.*（使）匆忙行事 & *n.* 匆忙
11. **pre-** [pri] *prefix* 在……之前

CH
2

From: calendarplanet@calendarplanet.com

To: all.subscribers@calendarplanet.com

Subject: Special Deals

Hi!

Here at Calendar Planet, we know the joy that calendars bring. Even in today's world when we can easily check the date on our smartphones, there's nothing quite like turning over a new month on a real calendar. Today only, we're offering our members these special deals:

Buy a film star calendar and **SAVE $2** by entering "CP2"

Buy a music star calendar and **SAVE $4** by entering "CP4"

Buy a sports star calendar and **SAVE $6** by entering "CP6"

Buy a towns & villages calendar and **SAVE $8** by entering "CP8"

The Calendar Planet Team

---

https:// www.calendarplanet.com

Customer Reviews

I have bought calendars from your company for many years and they have always been good quality. Actually, the calendar I chose this year is even better than usual! The images of my favorite tennis player, Hsieh Shu-Wei, are excellent. I look forward to turning them over every month. Your prices are also very good, and it was a nice idea to offer your regular customers an extra saving. I certainly will buy calendars from you again!

Robert

寄件者：	calendarplanet@calendarplanet.com
收件者：	all.subscribers@calendarplanet.com
主　旨：	特惠方案

嗨！

在月曆星球，我們知道月曆會帶來什麼樂趣。即便是在今天這個可以隨時在智慧型手機上查閱日期的世界裡，也沒有什麼比得上在實體月曆中翻到新的月份的樂趣。在此我們提供以下特惠方案給我們的會員，只有今天喔：

　　購買電影明星月曆時輸入 CP2 可**省下兩美元**
　　購買樂壇歌手月曆時輸入 CP4 可**省下四美元**
　　購買運動明星月曆時輸入 CP6 可**省下六美元**
　　購買城鄉美景月曆時輸入 CP8 可**省下八美元**

月曆星球團隊

---

https:// www.calendarplanet.com　－ □ ×

顧客評價

我已跟貴公司購買月曆多年，它們的品質一直都很好。事實上，我今年選購的月曆比往年買到的更好！我最喜歡的網球選手謝淑薇的照片超棒。我很期待每個月翻開新的一頁。你們的價格也非常實惠，提供老客戶額外折扣真不錯。我一定會再跟你們購買月曆！

羅伯特

<u>A</u> **1.** Why does the email talk about smartphones?

A. Many people use the calendar on their phones.

B. Many people shop for calendars on their phones.

C. The special deals are only available for phone orders.

D. The most popular calendar includes pictures of phones.

電子郵件中為什麼提及智慧型手機？

A. 許多人使用手機上的月曆。

B. 許多人在手機上購買月曆。

C. 特惠方案只適用於使用手機訂購的人。

D. 最受歡迎的月曆內有手機的照片。

理由

問題類型： 細節題

根據電子郵件內文第一段第二句 "Even in today's world when we can easily check the date on our smartphones..."（即便是在今天這個可以隨時在智慧型手機上查閱日期的世界裡……），得知 A 項應為正選。

<u>D</u> **2.** What do we discover about Robert?

A. He won't use Calendar Planet next year.

B. He rarely buys goods from online stores.

C. He plans to buy many different calendars.

D. He has shopped at Calendar Planet before.

關於羅伯特，我們發現哪件事？

A. 他明年不會再使用月曆星球。

B. 他很少在網路商店購物。

C. 他打算買很多不同的月曆。

D. 他以前曾在月曆星球購物。

理由

問題類型： 細節題

根據顧客評價第一句 "I have bought calendars from your company for many years..."（我已跟貴公司購買月曆多年……），得知 D 項應為正選。

<u>C</u> **3.** How much money did Robert save on his calendar?

A. Two dollars

B. Four dollars

C. Six dollars

D. Eight dollars

羅伯特購買月曆省下了多少錢？

A. 兩美元

B. 四美元

C. 六美元

D. 八美元

理由

問題類型：多文本整合題

根據顧客評價第三句 "The images of my favorite tennis player, Hsieh Shu-Wei, are excellent."（我最喜歡的網球選手謝淑薇的照片超棒。）及電子郵件內文特惠方案第三項 "Buy a sports star calendar and **SAVE $6** by entering "CP6" "（購買運動明星月曆時輸入 CP6 **可省下六美元**），得知 C 項應為正選。

🏷 重要單字片語

1. **calendar** [ˋkæləndɚ] *n.* 日曆；月曆
2. **planet** [ˋplænɪt] *n.* 行星，星球
3. **enter** [ˋɛntɚ] *vt.* （電腦）輸入；進入
4. **village** [ˋvɪlɪdʒ] *n.* 村莊；鄉村
5. **team** [tim] *n.* 團隊；（球）隊 & *vi.* 合作，聯手

6. **image** [ˋɪmɪdʒ] *n.* 影像，圖像；形象；意象
7. **saving** [ˋsevɪŋ] *n.* 省下的錢；存款（做此義時恆用複數）
8. **discover** [dɪsˋkʌvɚ] *vt.* 發現
9. **rarely** [ˋrɛrlɪ] *adv.* 極少地；罕見地

CH
2

From: mail@mailmail.com

To: pmcnulty@mailmail.com

Subject: Welcome

Paul,

Sorry I can't be there for your first day on the job, for I'm taking some personal leave. However, I know the rest of the mailmen will look after you. If you have any questions, please ask them. Please see below for when and where you need to be. It is important to stick to these times.

Time	Street
7:00 a.m.	Lake Road
7:30 a.m.	Hill Road
8:00 a.m.	East Main Street
8:30 a.m.	West Main Street

See you later in the week.

Jimmy

Dear Rhonda,

Thank you very much for your letter. It came as a nice surprise when the mailman delivered it before I went out for my regular walk at seven fifteen this morning. I am glad you are having fun in Australia. It is a great idea to take a break between studying and starting work to see the world. Your grandmother would be so proud of the confident young woman you have become. Stay safe over there and keep in touch. I look forward to seeing your pictures when you come back.

Love, Grandpa

寄件者：	mail@mailmail.com
收件者：	pmcnulty@mailmail.com
主　旨：	歡迎

保羅：

很抱歉你到職當天我無法到公司，因為那天我有事要請假。不過我知道其他郵差同仁會照顧你。如果你有任何問題就請教他們。請看下方這張是你的送信時間與地點列表。請務必遵守這些時間。

CH
2

時間	街道名
上午七點	湖泊路
上午七點三十分	小丘路
上午八點	東大街
上午八點三十分	西大街

這週稍後見。

吉米

親愛的朗達：

真是謝謝妳的來信。就在我今早照往常在七點十五分去散步之前，看到郵差送信來，真是一個驚喜。我很高興妳在澳洲玩得愉快。畢業後先休息一下看看外面的世界再開始工作是個好主意。妳的奶奶一定很驕傲妳成為一個充滿自信的女青年。妳在那邊要注意安全，也要跟我們保持聯繫。我期待等妳回來後看妳拍的照片。

愛妳的爺爺

B **1.** Who most likely is Jimmy?
    A. A worker in a paper factory
    B. The boss of a mail company
    C. An old university friend of Paul's
    D. One of Paul's regular customers

吉米最有可能是什麼人？
A. 造紙廠工人
B. 郵遞公司老闆
C. 保羅大學時期的老友
D. 保羅的常客之一

理由

問題類型： 推論題

第一封電子郵件內文主要述說寄件者 Jimmy（吉米）因故無法陪伴新到任的郵差 Paul（保羅），但同事會照應他，並且叮嚀他要按時將郵件送達指定地點。以如此的敘事口吻可推知 Jimmy 應是保羅的主管或是公司的老闆，得知 B 項應為正選。

D **2.** Why is Rhonda in Australia?
    A. She is starting a new job there.
    B. She is visiting her grandmother.
    C. She is studying for a degree there.
    D. She is visiting the country for fun.

朗達為什麼在澳洲？
A. 她在那裡開始新工作。
B. 她在探望她奶奶。
C. 她在那裡攻讀學位。
D. 她去那個國家遊玩。

理由

問題類型： 細節題

根據第二封信內文第三、四句 "I am glad you are having fun in Australia. It is a great idea to take a break between studying and starting work to see the world."（我很高興妳在澳洲玩得愉快。畢業後先休息一下看看外面的世界再開始工作是個好主意。），得知 D 項應為正選。

A **3.** Where does Rhonda's grandfather live?
    A. Lake Road
    B. Hill Road
    C. East Main Street
    D. West Main Street

朗達的爺爺住在哪裡？
A. 湖泊路
B. 小丘路
C. 東大街
D. 西大街

理由

問題類型： 多文本整合題

第二封信內文第二句敘述 "It came as a nice surprise when the mailman delivered it before I went out for my regular walk at seven fifteen this morning."（就在我今早照往常在七點十五分去散步之前，看到郵差送信來，真是一個驚喜。），而第一封電子郵件內的送信時間表中，在上述時間點之前的時間為上午七點，送達地點為 Lake Road（湖泊路），得知 A 項應為正選。

🏷 重要單字片語

1. **personal** [ˋpɝsənḷ] *a.* 個人的，私人的
   personal leave　事假

2. **mailman** [ˋmel͵mæn] *n.* 郵差，郵遞員
   〔美〕(= postman [ˋpostmən]〔英〕)
   （複數形為 mailmen [ˋmel͵mɛn]）

3. **stick to sth**　遵守 / 堅持某事物

4. **deliver** [dɪˋlɪvɚ] *vt. & vi.* 投遞，運送
   （信件、貨物等）

5. **take a break**　休息一下

6. **be proud of...**　以……為榮，為……
   感到自豪

7. **confident** [ˋkɑnfədənt] *a.* 有信心的，
   自信的

8. **keep / stay in touch (with sb)**
   （與某人）保持聯繫

9. **university** [͵junəˋvɝsətɪ] *n.* 大學

CH
2

國家圖書館出版品預行編目（CIP）資料

GEPT 新制全民英檢初級閱讀實戰力 Level
Up!：詳解本 / 賴世雄作. – 初版. – 臺北市：
常春藤有聲出版股份有限公司, 2021.09
面；　公分.
--（常春藤全民英檢系列；G53-2）
ISBN 978-986-06662-5-0（平裝）
1. 英語　2. 讀本
805.1892　　　　　　　　110014636

常春藤全民英檢系列【G53－2】

GEPT 新制全民英檢初級　閱讀實戰力 Level Up!
（詳解本）

總 編 審	賴世雄
終　　審	梁民康
執行編輯	許嘉華
編輯小組	施盈如・區光銳・Nick Roden・Brian Foden
設計組長	王玥琦
封面設計	胡毓芸
排版設計	林桂旭・王穎緁
法律顧問	北辰著作權事務所蕭雄淋律師
出 版 者	常春藤有聲出版股份有限公司
地　　址	臺北市忠孝西路一段 33 號 5 樓
電　　話	(02) 2331-7600
傳　　真	(02) 2381-0918
網　　址	www.ivy.com.tw
電子信箱	service@ivy.com.tw
郵政劃撥	19714777
戶　　名	常春藤有聲出版股份有限公司
定　　價	420 元（2 書）